She Makes the Dopeboys Go Crazy

B. Love

D1418067

Soar young girl. Soar.

This is a work of fiction. Names, characters, places and incidents either are products of the author's imagination or are used fictitiously. Any resemblance to actual events or locales or persons, living or dead, is entirely coincidental.

Meya

"So you gon' leave me like all them other suckas did, Anna Mae?"

That was the first thing I heard when I woke up. I had a bad ass habit of falling asleep with the TV on – especially when I was drinking. My head was throbbing so hard it felt like my brain had a heartbeat. I was laying on my stomach with my head turned towards my window. My hair was tossed all over my pillow.

I moved my body slightly but stopped when the pounding in my head got worse. That's when I noticed that the middle of my bed was pressed down. Like someone was sitting on it. Like someone was sitting on *my* fucking bed. I refused to believe a nigga had broken into Cedrick's baby girl's crib, so I opened my eyes and tried to see through my window; but the blinds were going in several different directions blocking my view.

I had three guns under my bed. One on the left side. One on the right side. One at the foot of the bed. My only hope was going to be punching whoever it was hard enough to discombobulate them, reach under my bed to grab a gun, and dead their ass. I inhaled deeply and shot up from the bed. My fist connected with his face and I reached for my gun, but his hand wrapped around my loose hair and he slung me back down on the bed.

"Yo, what the fuck is wrong with you, Me?" Salem yelled, wrapping his hands around my neck.

For a moment, everything went silent and I felt like I was about to pass the fuck out. My head was pounding even harder now. Between him grabbing my hair and yelling so loud the pain literally made me sick to my stomach. I closed my eyes and covered his hands with mine.

"Did you just punch me?" Salem asked as he shook me softly.

"Nigga, get the hell off of me. I didn't know it was you. The hell are you doing in my house anyway?"

"Your crazy ass called me last night and told me to be over here as soon as the sun came up."

"No, I didn't, Salem."

"Yes you did, Me. You called me at midnight and told me that you had something important to talk to me about. You told me to be here as soon as the sun came up."

I turned my head slightly to avoid his eyes. His eyes always did something to me. I fell for those eyes the first time I looked into them ten years ago. They were so dark, deep, and emotionless. He stared at me like he wanted me to give him everything he was lacking; and ever since I was a teenager I've wanted to.

Ten years ago, when I was sixteen, he tried to break into my home. He was homeless, his parents had been murdered, and instead of him going to foster care for a year until he was eighteen, he started living on the streets. He robbed niggas, did odd jobs, sold drugs, and did whatever else he could to come up on some coins.

I guess he heard about my pops and how much weight he had in the streets. For some reason, he thought it would be easy to steal from us. So, he tried to break into our home, but my dad caught him. He beat his ass real good and talked to him to figure out what could have possessed him to try and rob the biggest drug dealer in Memphis.

When he told my pops his life story, my dad felt bad for him. He got him some clothes, fed him, let him stay in the mother-in-law suite behind our house, and put him on his payroll.

Over the years, Salem went up in rank, and by the time my pops was locked up he was his second in command. Now, he oversees all of our drug shipments, while I handle the money. Not only am I my pops accountant, but I handle most of the accounts for the dealers in Memphis that are actually making money and want to make sure they don't have to worry about getting caught up with the IRS. Niggas who want to make sure they have money to live off of when they retire, or want to make sure their families will be straight should something happen to them come to me for my services.

I'd always had a crush on Salem Myers, but he never wanted to take it there with me when we were younger. He had too much fear, loyalty, and respect towards my father to cross that line with me; but right after my dad got locked up I got my chance to have him. We fucked around for a couple of months and I ended up giving him my virginity before he realized that he couldn't go through with it. He told me that my pops made him promise to look after me, and as good as my pops had been to him he felt like he was being disloyal. I respected that shit, but I hated his ass for it at the same time.

His hazelnut colored skin was so smooth it glowed. It was blemish and tattoo free, but his muscles gave him that bad boy look that I loved. He had a strong jaw line, skin colored lips, deep wavy hair and those eyes… those espresso brown eyes were so rich and so commanding… I was in love with those eyes. They were void of love and compassion, and the only time it looked as if they were filled with some type of emotion was when he was talking to me or my father.

I avoided those eyes now that he'd broken my heart. They either reminded me that he was heartless, or that I was one of the few people he actually cared about.

How crazy was that?

"Will you let me go?" I asked softly.

He stared at me for a few seconds before releasing me. When he did, I carefully sat up and made my way next to him. He handed me the bottle of water that was on my nightstand, my Tylenol, and a piece of gum.

"Your breath smells disgusting, Me."

"Ain't nobody tell you to be in here all up in my face," I mumbled opening the water.

"You told me, crazy ass girl." His hand rested on my thigh and I looked at him briefly before pushing it off. "So, what's up? What did you want to talk to me about?"

"I ain't want to talk to your ass about shit!" I yelled louder than I wanted to before massaging my temples.

"Who you yelling at?"

"You." My voice was lighter as I popped two Tylenols in my mouth.

I used to love this man. He used to be my best friend. Now, I hated to be anywhere near him. Not because I hated being with him, but because I loved being with him. As much as I wanted him, though, I knew he would never take it there with me again. That ate at me. It was like, I resented him more and more each time I saw him.

"A drunk mouth speaks sober thoughts. Obviously there was something on your mind. Don't shut down now."

I rolled my eyes and shook my head.

"Salem, go home. I don't remember anything that happened last night. I don't remember calling you. I don't remember what I could have possibly wanted to talk to you about."

"Us. You wanted to talk about us."

"Did I say that?"

"No."

"Then how do you…"

"Meya, you been giving me hell since…"

"Since you fucked me and left me alone?"

"You know it wasn't like that, baby. I couldn't do that to pops. I felt like I was sleeping with my sister."

"But I'm not your sister, Salem. I've never been your sister. I don't want to be your sister."

"What you wanna be then?"

His question caught me off guard. I sat my bottle of water down and considered several answers – none of them the truth.

"What you wanna be, Me? You wanna be my woman? You can't be. You know that. He would be devastated if we did that. I love you, more than you know, but we can't take it there. Had I known you were a virgin I wouldn't have even taken it there with you. I felt bad as hell about that. I'm sorry."

"I'm not."

I thought I said that in my brain, but when he chuckled and pulled my lips to his I realized I said it out loud.

His tongue opened my lips, and as much as I wanted to give him access, I couldn't. I pushed him away and scooted into the middle of my bed.

"You're confusing me," I admitted.

"I'm sorry. You know I want you. I can't help it."

"Then have me."

"I can't."

"Then get the fuck out."

"Meya…"

"Go, Salem. I'm tired of playing with your confused inconsistent ass."

"I'm not confused. I know what I want and I'm very clear about it. I also know what will and will not happen. I want you, but I'm not going to have you."

"Goodbye, Salem."

"I love you."

He stood and I laid down and turned my back to him.

"Don't worry about locking up behind you. Drop your key on the table on your way out."

"Girl, please. Get out your feelings. Pops asked me to look after you. Whether I do that as your friend, brother, lover, or enemy that's what I'm gonna do. And you bet not get the locks changed again either. And don't be late for the meeting."

I flipped him off and closed my eyes, hoping I could get at least one hour of sleep before having to get up and get ready for the weekly meeting.

Katara

My cousin was one of the baddest living. She could stand in front of a hundred men, look sweet as pie, and shoot her gun before any of them had a chance to pull theirs. Her skin was a pretty golden brown shade. She had high pointy cheek bones, thick curly hair, and tight almond eyes. That body of hers... she was slim thick and toned as hell. As pretty as she was, though, her attitude was just as reckless and grimy.

That came from being raised by my uncle Ced. When her mother was pregnant with her, her family didn't approve of uncle Ced. They said they didn't want their family to be tainted by his lifestyle. So, when Meya was born, uncle Ced paid her mother and her family off and got sole custody of Me. I think not having her mother around bothered her when she was a teenager and old enough to notice her mother's presence was lacking, but eventually she got over that shit.

And although we all knew why her mother left, Uncle Ced made us all promise to never tell Meya. He didn't want her to grow up feeling like she wasn't loved or wanted. Like her mother valued money and her parents more than Meya.

Uncle Ced wanted Me to be raised like a Queen. A Queen who knew her worth. One who was confident and fully aware of her value. So... we never spoke of her mother or the reason she left. Uncle Ced gave Me everything she wanted and needed and left no room for her to miss a mother she never knew.

Even as a kid she clung to men more than women. Really, the only chick she fucked with was me. She didn't show her emotions. She didn't want love or commitment. She messed around with multiple niggas just to avoid catching feelings – especially after what went down with her and Salem. She didn't think I noticed that things had changed between them, but I did. When I confronted her about it she broke down and told me everything.

Her little escapade with him turned her into this... careless, reckless, unemotional man-eater. She used niggas for money, sex, and companionship when she wanted them, then quickly dismissed them when she was done. It was like, she would literally drain a nigga and feed off of his ass and just toss him to the side. Me would say that her change within had nothing to do with losing her father and Salem, but I knew better than to believe that.

I remember one night – we went to a concert here in Memphis. She had the biggest crush on this rapper here named Pete. While he performed, she sung every lyric to his songs. Her ass was rocking with him harder than his niggas, and he took notice of that shit. When the show was over, he told her to come back stage.

I guess he thought she was gone be on some groupie fuck shit; but her ass ended up walking out of his dressing room with ten stacks and wet panties from him eating her until she came. He begged her for her number, she gave him mine, and she's been avoiding his ass ever since.

You know how niggas do, though, it's okay for them to not want you... but if you turn them down they make it their life's mission to get you and make you want them. That's what she dealt with on a daily basis. Throngs of nigga's, especially local dope boys, begging for her attention and affection. She knew she made the dope boys go crazy... and she fed off that shit!!

She would laugh in their face with promises of love one day, knowing her ass wasn't capable of that shit. Not with any of them anyway.

She walked into the warehouse and I swear *all* conversations ceased at the sound of her heels stabbing the floor. Everyone looked at her, and she blushed and looked at me. Normally, women weren't allowed to attend the meetings, especially women who weren't involved with the business, but I was her assistant, so wherever she was I was most times.

Salem stood and walked towards her. She mugged him and met him halfway. As much as she hated him, she tried her hardest not to let it show in front of the team. She didn't want her personal shit to affect business, nor did she want anyone on the team to find out her weakness. We trusted our team, but we took no chances with them. There was always a chance for a Judas to pop up, so the less they knew about Salem and Meya the better.

He stood in front of her and looked down at her. I tried to read his lips to see what he was saying to her. Whatever it was, it must not have been something she liked because her eyes kept tightening and her breathing accelerated. Her chest was rising and falling hard and quick, and then she closed her eyes and took a step back. Biting her lip, she turned her side to him and looked at the men seated around the table.

"One of you niggas a snake," she mumbled walking towards the table slowly. She rested her palms on the table and looked every one of them in their eyes. "After everything my father has done for you niggas... you mean to tell me that one of y'all got the nerve to work with the enemy?"

Salem walked behind her and put his hand on her back. She looked at him and stood upright.

"This nigga... they call him the John the Baptist of the streets because he prepares the way for his boss to come in and take over territories. Which one of you thought it would be cool to tell him about our organization?"

None of them answered and she laughed.

"Aight, y'all don't wanna talk? Nobody wants to come forward? Fuck it, then. Salem, kill all of them. I'm not about to waste my time and energy trying to find out who gave away confidential information. I know you niggas know. Y'all wanna be loyal to one another instead of the ones that feed you? Cool. Y'all can die together too."

She turned to walk away and Carlos stopped her.

"Fuck that, Me. I ain't losing my life for naine nigga. I'll tell you who did it," he blurted out.

"Who was it?" Salem asked as Meya turned back around.

"It was Juan."

"Nigga!" Juan yelled jumping from his seat.

Salem pulled his gun and aimed it at Juan. He looked back at Meya and she nodded. Without blinking or flinching, one bullet went into Juan's head, and then Carlos'.

Salem put his gun back at his waist and spoke.

"You niggas wanna be loyal, be loyal to Ced, Meya, and Salem. You niggas snitch, it's death for you because we still wouldn't be able to trust your loyalty. So, if you don't want a bullet to the head, be loyal to Ced, Meya, and Salem. Nobody else. Ride for each other like the family we are, but you are to put no one on this team or against this team above Ced, Meya, and Salem. You don't even put yourselves above us. Why? Because we take care of you motherfuckers better than y'all could ever take care of yourselves. Cross us if you want to."

Everyone's eyes were focused on Salem, but I was watching my girl. She was looking at Salem like she wanted to rip off his clothes and have her way with him right here and right now! Taking a step back, she looked at me and I chuckled. She nodded at me before walking out. Her ass was about to go and call one of her niggas to put out the fire Salem had started within her.

John the Baptist

Ambitionz Az A Ridah was blasting from my Beats Pill. Anytime I was preparing to go in for a mission I listened to Pac. For this mission, I was listening to *All Eyez on Me*. I had been back in Memphis for about a week before I received word on who I was supposed to go after. When I left six years ago, it was to live a better life. I ended up moving to Richmond and linking up with some more streets niggas. Swear it felt like I was born and built for this shit. It didn't matter how hard I tried to be a good, straight, and legal working man… the streets always found a way to pull me back in.

Now, I was working as what you could call a cleanup man. Basically, I go to different cities and neighborhoods and clean up any competition the person who hired me has. When I take care of that competition, my client comes in and sets up shop. Sometimes, taking care of the competition was as simple as paying them off, or threatening them… other times it meant ending their lives and their reign in that city. When my current client told me that he wanted me to take care of a female, I laughed at his ass. I couldn't understand why he would need my help for that; but when he told me who that female was, and who her father was, I understood.

Cedrick and Meya James were nothing to fuck with, especially with Salem Myers on their team. I was never one to back down from a challenge, so I accepted the job, but I was going to have to put more time into this one than I ever had before. And for the first time… I may need to call in a second line of help just in case shit went left – Omen.

Meya

Nothing relaxed me more than weed and head. After a rough day I couldn't wait to get home to shower, pour me a glass of wine, and roll me a blunt. The shit with Juan and Carlos really messed with my mental, though. It always cuts you deep when you find out niggas on your team have betrayed you and been disloyal. I'd found out all that I could about this John the Baptist nigga, but really, that wasn't much. He's like a fucking ghost. Most times you don't see him coming until it's too late, and when he hits you... there are no witnesses. Those still living can't identify him. Word on the street was that every business he came to clean up shut down, but I was about to put an end to that shit.

When I got home, I called my number one friend, Kendrick. He was a pretty ass dread head I met at the gym. He's a personal trainer, and he offered to give me two free sessions. I took them, and he's been working me out ever since. I loved looking down at him. Both of his ears were pierced, his thick eyebrows looked like they were naturally arched, his lips were full and pink, and his skin was a tad darker than cashews.

He was kneeling before me, with my legs spread... just staring at me. I hit my blunt and blew the smoke in his mouth. After he exhaled it he pulled me to the edge of the couch and kissed my clit through my panties. My doorknob started jiggling and I threw my head back in frustration.

Salem.

"Didn't I tell you to leave your key here?" I asked as he walked in without knocking or ringing the doorbell.

Kendrick stood and sat next to me. Salem stared at Kendrick, and Kendrick stared back.

"Say..."

"Who the fuck is this nigga?"

"Don't come in my house questioning me."

His eyes met mine and I looked away.

"Who you?" he asked Kendrick.

Kendrick chuckled and stood. "I'm Kendrick, how are you?" Kendrick extended his hand.

Salem looked from it to me. He nodded and sat where Kendrick was first seated.

"Can you give us some privacy, Kendrick?"

"Nigga, you can't just dismiss my company. I was in the middle of something."

"I don't give a fuck. He need to leave."

"No, *you* need to leave."

"Me, I'm not in the mood to play with your ass tonight. Say goodnight to your friend. You don't need to have no niggas up in here anyway."

I chuckled angrily and licked my lips.

"Kendrick, I'm sorry, my *brother* is very rude."

"Oh, so now I'm your brother? You ain't wanna be my sister this morning, but since this nigga here we related?"

I stood and wrapped my arm around Kendrick's.

"Can I come by tonight and stay til the morning?" I asked as I walked him to my door. "I need to nut."

He chuckled and squeezed my ass. Besides Salem, I'd never let any other nigga fuck me, but I'd let plenty eat the pussy. Kendrick, however, was the only nigga besides Salem I'd consider letting inside of me. Fully. He was nice and sweet and patient and that body...

"You know I got you, Me."

"Thank you, you're one of the few niggas that don't question me. You accept me and you don't expect shit from me. I appreciate that."

"I know what's up. I know what you want and need from me. I ain't no fool. I'm not gone expect something you haven't offered to give."

His arms wrapped around my waist, and he pulled me into him. Just the feel of his dick against me had me wanting to run out my own house with this nigga to get a quickie.

"Meya!" Salem's country ass was working every damn nerve I had!!

"Here I come!" I yelled getting irritated all over again.

"Take care of your business, Me. You know where to find me."

I nodded as he released me. Once I locked up behind him I walked back into my den and stared at Salem with my arms crossed.

"Who was that?" He pushed my arms down and sat me next to him.

"Kendrick."

"Okay, who is Kendrick?"

"Why does it matter?"

He stared at me and I looked away.

"Why you can't look at me no more?"

"What do you want, Say?"

"Answer my question, Meya. And why that nigga calling you Me? Make that nigga call you Meya. That nickname ain't for everybody. *You* ain't for everybody."

"You let Katara call me that."

"Because her ass don't listen, and she family. I don't call you that because of your name. We're not committed so I can't say you belong to me... but gahdamn you *are* me. That's why I call you that shit. Let another nigga call you that."

I shook my head and tossed my leg over his lap. His hand covered my thigh, and I covered his hand with mine.

"Now answer my question, Me."

"Because I can't take it."

"What you mean you can't take it?"

His voice had softened, and his thumb was caressing my thigh so softly chills pierced my skin.

"You know I love you."

"And I love you. I kill for you. I go to war for your ass on a daily basis, Me."

"I know." My eyes watered and I picked my blunt back up. I refused to get in my feelings over this nigga. "But that's not the kind of love I need from you."

My phone started ringing, so I grabbed it, but he snatched it from my hand and pressed ignore.

"You know you can't answer that while you talking to me. Call them back later."

"You so demanding. You act like you my nigga or some. My daddy don't even trip the way you do."

He chuckled and ran his hand up my thigh. My legs opened unwillingly and I closed them quickly.

"Salem, what do you want?"

"You. You know seeing you boss up on niggas always turns me on. And I know you wanted me too. That's why you left the warehouse."

"Salem, gone on with this bullshit."

"Show me you love me."

I couldn't even reply because his hand entangled with my hair and he pulled my face to his. My mouth opened slightly, and his tongue licked the edge of my mouth slowly.

"Touch my tongue," he mumbled.

I bit my lip and watched as he opened his mouth and stuck his tongue out. Slowly, I ran my tongue around his until he closed his lips and sucked it. I pulled away, but he gripped my hair tighter and pulled me back into him. He pecked my lips gently and with so much care and passion I moaned. His tongue went inside of my mouth and I gave in.

Wrapping my hands around his neck, I savored the feel of his hands running down my neck to my breasts. His tongue brushing against mine. His hands squeezing my breasts. His lips sucking mine.

"Take this pussy," I pleaded, trying to get on my knees so he could hit it from the back, but he stopped me.

"What you doing?" Salem lifted my dress over my head.

"I don't want to look at you," I confessed.

"I want you to look me in my eyes while I get in your pussy."

"Salem…" I whined trying not to lose control.

I wanted this. I wanted him. So fucking bad. But I knew looking into his eyes would send me over the edge. I didn't want him to make love to me, that would only make this harder. I needed him to fuck me.

"Shhh." He put his finger over my lips, then pulled my panties down. Salem kneeled before me and pushed my legs back. Once he spread my pussy lips he looked up at me and asked, "You know I love you, Me, right?"

I closed my eyes and inhaled deeply as his tongue slowly went up and down my clit. Just the feel of his tongue against me was about to send me in. We hadn't had sex in years, and no other man had satisfied me or gave me the desire to see if he would fit me the way Salem did. He worked my clit slowly and then side to side so fast my legs shook. I held them as he sucked my clit continuously.

"Shit, Salem," I moaned.

He was kissing my clit like he had just finished kissing my lips.

"You giving niggas what's mine?" He stuck his middle finger inside of me. I gripped his head and squeezed. "Answer me," he mumbled before sucking and slurping my clit.

"You don't want it," I moaned trying to push him away.

It was starting to feel too good. He massaged my thighs and I shuddered.

"Stop, Say, I'm about to cum," I pleaded, but that just made him work me even harder.

He lifted himself from my clit and started putting ultimate pressure on my G-spot. Pushing his fingers against it in that way that only he knew how to do. Fuck it... I didn't want it to be true... but...

"Fuck, Salem. No one else can please me or get on my damn nerves the way you do."

"You want this pussy to cum, you bring it here. Don't give it to no other niggas," he ordered as I erupted and squirted all over his hand and chest.

I pushed him away from me and tried to compose myself, but I knew that wasn't going to be happening any time soon when he started to undress. I admired his smooth chocolate skin and wondered if I could cut him out of my life completely. There was no way in hell I could handle him giving another woman what he was about to give me.

His hands wrapped around my waist and he kissed my stomach so sweetly. He positioned himself in between my thighs and wrapped my legs around his waist. My eyes lowered and I watched him run the head of his dick up and down my clit.

Salem eased himself inside of me inch by inch, and we both held our breath until he was in completely. I know this shit is going to sound corny, but the second he slid inside of me, I swear it felt like my heart worked again. He began to move inside of me and I closed my eyes as I ran my hands up and down his chest.

"Look at me," he commanded as he stroked me slow and deep.

I opened my eyes and saw love in his. I saw passion in his.

"Salem," I muttered as he wrapped his hands around my neck and moaned.

The hisses that erupted from my mouth, juice that fell from my insides, and smacking that filled the room was all consuming. He took my hands into his and lifted them over my head, kissing me and moaning deeply. So deeply. My lips and legs began to quiver and I succumbed to my second orgasm.

There was something about a man, no, there was something about *this* man, kissing me with the same slow speed that he stroked me and moaning to show his pleasure that did something to me. As hard and tough as he was, in this intimate moment he was open, vulnerable, and soft and that made me feel open, vulnerable, and soft.

Salem made me feel like a woman. Forget who my father is. Forget the weight I hold in the streets. Salem made me feel like a woman. Salem made me feel. No other man had that power. He released my hands and I quickly wrapped them around his neck as he plunged even deeper inside of me. So deep I couldn't even speak. All I could do was hold him tighter and allow him to have his way with me.

His movements began to speed up, and his strokes went from long and deep to short and quick. He was torturing my G spot while avoiding his own climax. My pussy began to clench him again. Heat was radiating from my walls. He flung his head back and bit down on his lip.

"Meya," he moaned gripping my thighs and squeezing tightly.

"Stop playing with my spot and go deep," I pleaded as I fought yet another orgasm. My G-spot was swelling and gripping him tighter and tighter.

"You 'bout to make me cum, baby."

"Cum, Salem. Let me feel it."

"You gone have my baby?" he asked speeding up his movements.

"Hell nah, nigga. You don't even wanna be my man. What makes you think I wanna be tied to you for life?"

"You tied to me for life regardless, Me. You ain't figured that out yet?"

He started going deeper, brushing against my clit, and anything I wanted to say left my brain as I came and felt his hot cum shooting straight through me.

Katara

Something was different about Me when she walked out of her house this morning. Her walk was different. Usually, when she walked she held her head high like the Queen she was, but this morning her head was hanging. She got in my car and we hardly talked on our way to visit uncle Ced.

After we were searched and escorted to the visitation room I looked at her and asked, "So, we just gone ignore what's going on, or you gone tell me what happened?"

"Nothing happened," she mumbled looking towards the floor.

"Don't lie to me, Meya. I can tell when you're in your feelings. And the only time you get in your feelings is when something happens with uncle Ced or Salem. So, what happened?"

She exhaled a hard breath and looked at me.

"He came over last night."

"Okay, what happened? I thought you were with Kendrick last night?"

"I was. He put him out."

I chuckled. Salem was crazy and possessive as hell. It didn't matter how much he pushed Meya away, he refused to let her be with anybody else.

"What happened after he put him out?"

"Katara…" She grabbed my hand and looked into my eyes. "He made love to me. He tied his fucking soul even tighter to mine."

I removed my hand and sat up straight.

"Meya, why would you do that? You know how you feel about that nigga. Why would you put yourself in the position to be even more crazy by having sex with him?"

She shrugged and shook her head.

"What was I supposed to do? I wanted him. I love him. I hate him, but I love him."

"So, what? Y'all in a relationship now or some shit?"

"Nah. Ain't nothing changed."

I shook my head and sighed. I didn't even want to talk about that shit anymore.

"Does uncle Ced know about this John the Baptist nigga?"

"Nah, that's what he wants to talk about now. He called me yesterday and was basically like stand down. He wants Say to handle him, but you know I can't do that."

"Technically, you're his accountant, Me. You pretty with your pistol, but I heard this nigga don't play around."

"Exactly. I'm not going to let Salem go into this by himself; especially for me and my pops."

"He won't be by himself. He's got a whole team behind him."

"I hear you."

When she said that, that usually meant she wasn't changing her mind and she didn't want to talk about that subject anymore.

"So, what's up with you, Kat? What's going on in your life besides having to deal with my bullshit?"

I smiled and sat back in my seat.

"Nothing. You know I'm going back to school this fall. Other than that, I'm just chilling."

"No boo thang yet?"

"Nah, not yet. We be looking mean when we're out in these streets, so niggas don't be tryna talk to me."

"We can't help we got resting bitch face syndrome."

"Mane, the struggle is real. I'm not worried about it, though. The right man will come along and be able to see through that."

"Long as you know. Don't settle either. We need to go away for a girls' trip. When this John the Baptist shit is settled we need to just... get away."

"You know I'm down. I'll start looking up some places. And I am *not* sharing a room with you anymore."

"What? Why?"

"Don't play innocent. Last time we went to Miami you brought that nigga back to the room and had him eating you like I wasn't even in the room. Then, when you put the nigga out I had to hear his yelling because you didn't return the favor."

She chuckled and crossed her legs.

"I told him what was going to happen when we got back to the room. I don't know why he thought I was going to change my mind. These niggas ain't good for giving me nothing but money and head. If I need anything else, I know who to get it from."

"Who Say?"

"No Kendrick. He's my official fuck buddy. We ain't took it all the way yet, but we got tested together. I don't let these other niggas slide in with nothing but their tongue."

"So, what you call what you did with Salem last night?"

The doors of the visitation room swung open and uncle Ced was first in line.

"Salem ain't on the same level as these other niggas. Say is my heart. No one has access to it but him. And after last night, I don't know if they'll have access to my body either."

"What? Meya the man-eater is considering changing her ways?"

"I don't know. I'm not going to lock myself up while he's out roaming free. I don't know. We'll see."

I nodded and we stood to embrace uncle Ced. This I had to see to believe.

John the Baptist

Word began to spread about Salem and Meya's execution of Juan and Carlos. With them knowing about my presence lingering in their camp, I had to regroup and consider a different plan of attack. In order for me to attack properly I was going to have to follow them both and find their weaknesses and strike there, leaving them with two options – bow out gracefully and make room for my client, or lose their product, team, money, and one of them their lives... forcing the other to have to restart from the ground up... just not in Memphis.

I called Omen and told him to meet up with me, and he was just as surprised to be receiving the call as I was to have been making it. Omen was the first nigga that started me on this street shit in Memphis. He had a reputation for being unfuckwithable, but one night he was caught slipping. I was there to help him. And he offered me a job as his main muscle.

That led to other things. He taught me all he wanted me to know, and I learned firsthand that saying about never going beyond your teacher was only true when your teacher held information back from you. I felt like if I ever wanted to be my own boss I would have to remove myself from his grip.

What Jay Z say? Until you're on your own you can't be free.

How you a boss but you gotta ask your boss for permission?

Asking if you may do this and do that like it's fucking Cinco de Mayo around this bitch.

I was over that shit.

So, I stepped out on my own. We were still cool. He was actually the first client I had. Then, he was the reason I received more. But I just needed to be on my own, feel me? I found out later that he held back because he didn't really want me in the streets. My mentor came to him as a man and asked him not to show me too much of that lifestyle. That he was working hard to keep me out of it, and he didn't want Omen or anyone else pulling me in.

I was my own man by that age, though, so my mentor knew I was going to get into what I wanted to get into. But Omen kept his promise to my mentor. He only let me get so deep in the streets.

I hit 'em up, though, and he came through. I'd just finished telling him about Cedrick, Meya, and Salem and he was shaking his head like I was in over mine.

"You're good at what you do," he started. And even though he grew silent I knew there was more on his mind. Sure enough, he started talking again. "But there's a dynamic between Salem and Meya that you've miscalculated by taking this job."

"What dynamic is that?"

Omen stood and walked over to the window that gave a decent view of my backyard.

"I watched Cedrick train them. Groom them both. He groomed them to have a power relationship. They love each other, yea. They respect each other, yea. But what pulls them together most is the power they grew up feeding each other. In most relationships of power, one person has more power over the other. Meya and Salem were trained to literally be each other's greatest threats and greatest strengths.

No one can come between them but each other. They alone have the power to lift each other up and tear each other down. They're each other's strengths and weaknesses. That's why they've expanded Cedrick's business as well as they have. I'm not saying it's going to be impossible to hit and get out without them finding you, but I will say this will be the hardest job you've ever had if you don't execute it properly."

"What's the key?"

He obviously knew more about them than I did and how they operated. I was never too proud to gain knowledge or help when needed. Omen looked back at me and smiled.

"You will only have one chance to strike, and when you do... it has to be lethal. It has to be something that will destroy the power they've given each other for years. You're taking the wrong route. This is a business hit, but you don't hit the business. They will *always* regroup. You must hit them personally. Their personal relationship is the only thing that will hinder their power and business relationship with each other. Put the business to the side and look into their personal lives. That's the only way you will be successful. Use business hits as a distraction if you must... but your target must be their personal relationship."

I nodded and released a deep breath. Going into their personal lives never would have crossed my mind simply because I would have guessed they would have had their personal lives on lock. But with the way Omen broke it down... I guess that makes a lot of sense. They do have their business sewn up. Their personal lives would be my best route in.

Meya

I can't lie, this nigga that approached Katara was pretty as hell. It's routine for us to scope the place out as soon as we arrive. When we made it to L.O.V.E I saw him in the cut and his eyes landed on Katara immediately. That's my goon, and I always have her back, so I told her I was going to the bathroom but made a beeline for him instead.

I snatched him and pulled him to the back and got a feel for him before he even approached her. He wasn't into any crazy shit and he wasn't in the streets so I gave him a pass to get at her. I gave him her number before he approached her because Kat more than likely wasn't going to give it to him unless his game was super strong.

His light skinned ass sauntered over to her all slow and it took all of my G and my strength not to burst into laughter. Swear it was the cutest shit I'd ever seen. She grabbed my hand and squeezed tightly like she couldn't believe he was coming for her. Kat is gorgeous, but between having to grow up with my pops as her uncle and his crazy ass brother for her father, her attitude was just as savage as mine.

She's more feminine and loving because she actually had her mother around, though. With light brown skin, long natural hair that's shaped in a heart shaped afro, chubby cheeks, bright eyes and a beautiful smile my boo be killing these niggas; but her ass be walking around with the meanest mug. I do the shit too, but they expect it from me because of who I am. Her smile, though, when she finally does smile… it literally lights up the whole room, and I'm not just saying that because she's my blood.

Katara's smile could make any man melt.

So when she finally looked at the nigga and smiled, he smiled and patted his heart like she had just blessed his soul. He grabbed her hand and pulled her to the side. That ain't stop me from being nosey though. We go to war over Kat. Point blank period. He looked like a pretty good dude, though.

He was a tall ass light skinned nigga with a low fade, low beard, brown and pink full lips, and flat tight dark eyes. He had that light skinned nigga swag. That look in his eyes that he just knew he was the shit. I shook my head and smiled as he wrapped his arm around her waist. Her crazy ass looked at him like he was crazy as she tried to push his hand away, but he kept it there and stepped closer to her.

Her hands went up in a don't shoot motion, but she relaxed and rested them on his chest. I chuckled even harder as I picked up my drink, but my smile fell immediately when I saw a nigga that looked like Salem out of the corner of my eye.

It couldn't have been Salem, because this nigga was with a bitch. In public. Like I wasn't crazy. I would never go out with a nigga in public on the strength of my dysfunctional relationship and respect for him, so I knew it wasn't Salem. I just knew it wasn't Salem. I just knew he wasn't out in public with a bitch.

I just knew it wasn't fucking Salem.

Not after I'd just given myself to him and let him plant his seeds in me. I chugged the rest of my drink, closed my eyes, and inhaled deeply before opening them and turning to the side. Sure enough, it was Salem.

I rubbed my hands together and stood. Kat looked my way and removed herself from her new boo thang's grip. She started walking towards me, but I held my hand up and stopped her. She looked towards the direction of my eyes and saw Salem. She cursed and walked towards me.

"Don't do nothing stupid, Me. It's too many people and too many phones in here. That shit gone be on Facebook as soon as we leave, and if the pigs get it that's it for your ass. All they waiting for is a reason to arrest you and Salem for the simplest thing so they can have access to all accounts, homes, and warehouses. Be smart, Meya."

I looked at her and nodded. She was right, but I didn't give a fuck. I tried to walk towards him, but she grabbed me by my arm.

"Don't do it, Me."

"I just wanna go talk to him."

"Bullshit. Don't do it, Meya."

"Let me go, Kat."

She released me and walked behind me as I walked towards Salem. My hand reached in my purse and Kat grabbed me again.

"Are you fucking crazy? You bet not pull that shit out in here, Me!"

"Gone back up there with that nigga. I got this."

"Meya, please."

I pulled myself away from her and continued my pursuit. His eyes found me and he stood and pulled his friend up immediately. He grabbed her by her arm and started walking towards the exit.

"Don't run, nigga!" I yelled walking faster.

"Go home, Me. Not here," he yelled back as he put her in front of him.

They made it outside and I was right behind them.

"Salem!" I yelled as he pushed her into his car.

He looked at me briefly with regret in his eyes, but his eyebrows wrinkled in anger. I just knew this nigga wasn't about to try and cop an attitude with me. I put my hand back in my purse to pull out the .22 he gave me for my birthday and shoot his tires out so he wouldn't be able to leave, but a strong hand grabbed me by my wrist and stopped me.

I looked to the side and locked eyes with a nigga I'd never seen before. It was dark out, so I couldn't make out all of his features, but I could tell he was attractive.

"Don't do it, Queen. **Never let a nigga bring you out of yourself.** You don't love the one you love. You love the one that loves you. Obviously that nigga don't love you if he's here with someone else. Let his ass leave."

I released the hold I had on my gun and let my purse fall back to my side. I was expecting him to let my wrist go but he didn't.

"Better?" he asked in a deep and rich voice. It immediately made me think about Kevin Gates.

I nodded and swallowed hard.

"Come back inside with me and let me buy you a drink. Give that nigga something to think about when he gets home."

He smiled and his teeth were so white and perfect in shape my nipples hardened. I was over this lounge shit for the night. I looked back to see if Kat was still outside and she was.

"Come here, Kat," I called as I watched Salem try and walk towards me.

I shook my head no and put my hand up and made a gun. I pulled my thumb trigger and his fists balled in anger. If he didn't want me to act a fool, his best bet was to leave me the hell alone while I was *trying* to behave. The nigga that was holding me grabbed my chin and pulled my attention to him.

"What I just say?"

Ole boy couldn't have known who I was to be handling me this way. For some reason, though, I didn't want to tell him. I just submitted and did as he said. I turned my back to Salem and turned my attention to Kat.

"I'm finna head out with this nigga. Get a picture of his license and tags. Take a picture of us together. If you don't hear from me in the morning you know what to do," I looked at him and asked, "What's your name?"

"Nasir. Nasir Patterson."

His hand cupped mine and he pulled it to his lips to kiss.

"Meya James. You wanna kick it with me for a little while to keep me out of trouble?"

Instead of answering verbally he pulled his wallet out and handed Kat his license. As she took a picture of it he looked me up and down, and for the first time in my life... I was insecure under a man's stare.

"Aight, y'all look at the camera," Kat instructed.

We did and she took a picture of us. When we were done he led us to his car and she took a picture of his tags.

"Text me and let me know where you end up," she said hugging me.

"I will. Have fun with light skinned. Don't let this ruin your night."

"Yea, we'll see."

We walked her back to the front doors of L.O.V.E and then he walked me to my car. Nasir opened the door for me and said, "Follow me."

I nodded and pulled my car around to where he was parked. My phone began to vibrate in my purse and I groaned. Couldn't be nobody but Salem. Nasir started his car and headed out of the parking lot. Once we were on the street and headed out I pulled my phone out.

"Yea?" I spoke.

"Where you going? I know you ain't leaving with that nigga? Where you know him from?" Salem asked me in one breath.

I started to hang up in his face, but I wanted to get under his skin.

"Don't worry about me. You weren't worried about what I was doing tonight when you decided to come out with that bitch."

"Meya, damn mane, we not together. You can't be beating bitches every time you see me with one."

"Then don't let me see you with one!" I yelled. "The fuck you out in public with her for anyway?"

"She got tired of us always being in the house. She wanted to go out."

"You fucking her?"

"Nah. I wouldn't have made love to you if I was fucking her."

"So you like her then?" He remained silent and that shit made my heart ache. He knew I couldn't handle watching him be with someone else, but since he obviously didn't care about my feelings I was on the verge of saying fuck his. "Salem!"

"She cool, Meya. I ain't saying I'm gonna be with her or some shit like that. I'm just kicking it with her. I'm tired of fucking around with all these random bitches. I'm ready to settle down, and she's a good contender."

"So, what the fuck am I, Salem?"

"My heart. You my day by day, Me. You know we can't be together, but you got my heart, baby. This chick and every other woman I fuck with know they don't have access to my heart. That's all yours." His chick made some type of nose in the background and he told her to shut up before he finished talking to me. "You who I run with, Me. You know that. We go beyond titles and shit."

"Fuck you, Salem. Do you and Ima do me."

"You can do you, but you bet not be doing no niggas. Get his ass killed if you want to."

I disconnected the call and beat my head against the headrest gently. This nigga had a hold on me, but Nasir was right... you gotta love the one that loves you. There was no point in me holding on to whatever this was that I had with Salem when it was clear that we would never be more than just friends.

Katara

When I walked back into the longue I looked over at our VIP table and didn't see Ricardo. He probably thought I didn't want to talk to him anymore, but family came first so I had to ride with Meya. When I saw Salem sitting next to some chick anything I was trying to build with him had to be put on hold. Meya had no problem acting a fool over Salem, and Salem had no problem acting a fool over Meya. Swear I hate their asses sometimes.

They either need to get together or just leave each other the hell alone. I walked back outside and headed for my car, but I heard Ricardo's voice and I stopped dead in my tracks.

"You gone leave without saying goodbye?" I heard the smile in his voice.

I smiled and turned around.

"I was coming back to say goodbye, but I didn't see you."

"Yea, I was talking to one of my niggas. Where your girl at?"

"She's gone."

"Everything good?"

"Yea, I guess."

"Doe, you heading out?"

Ricardo turned around and looked at the man that was talking to him.

"Yea, I'm finna grab a bite to eat with lil mama. I'll get up with you later."

He turned back around to me and I chuckled.

"Doe?" I asked.

"Yea, Ion like my name so everybody calls me Doe."

"I like your name. It's cute."

He nodded and wrapped his arm around my waist. He had a bad habit of not being able to keep his hands to himself.

"You can call me whatever you want, Beautiful. I'm hungry as hell, though. You riding with me?"

Meya's words replayed in my head. Normally I would say no, but I agreed to having a late dinner with Ricardo.

"I'll follow you out."

∞

Ricardo led me clear across town to Midtown for dinner. I wasn't expecting there to be too many places open around this time of night, but we went to a tiny tucked away soul food café. We ended up sitting outside for about thirty minutes before an older man appeared, unlocked the door, and let us in.

I watched as the older man and Ricardo talked quietly by the front door, then the older man went back to the kitchen and Ricardo came and sat next to me.

"What's up?" I asked him.

"Nothing. That's my uncle."

"You made him come and open his restaurant just to have a late dinner with me?"

Ricardo shrugged and grabbed my hand under the table. It was on my leg, so the feel of his knuckles on my thigh sent shivers all through my body.

"He makes the best fried catfish."

I tried to casually pull my hand from his, but he held it tighter and smiled.

"Why you tryna get away from me already, Katara?"

"I just don't understand why you think it's okay to keep touching all on me, Ricardo."

"You don't want me touching you?"

My body betrayed me. My pussy leaked. My nipples hardened. His voice had lowered an octave and it was so damn desperate and needy. But my mind was screaming *hell no*! So, instead of listening to my body that was slowly weakening under his spell, I listened to my mind.

"Nope. I don't know you well enough to be giving you permission to touch me. Not that you ask for permission anyway."

"I don't need permission to touch what's mine."

"But I'm not yours."

"Yes you are."

"No I'm not."

"Yes you are."

"No I'm not."

"Yes you are."

"No I'm…"

His free hand wrapped around my hair and he pulled my face close to his. He didn't kiss me like I thought he would. He just... pulled me so close had either of us licked our lips we'd touch. So close I felt his breath on my nose. So close I could smell the peppermint on his breath.

"Katara, I'm not going to play with you. You want me, just as much as I want you. Don't be afraid to act on that shit because I promise you I will. I *am*. If you can't handle that let me know and we can end this now. Otherwise, I'm holding your hand. I'm wrapping my arm around your waist. I'm kissing these pretty ass lips. I'm smacking the shit out of that ass. And I'm doing whatever the hell else I wanna do to you. Whatever you want me to do to you. Got me?"

Before I could respond he was releasing me and sitting back in his seat. My breath came out hard as I grabbed his hand and pulled it back to my thigh. He smiled and kissed my cheek and neck until I pushed him away.

"You lucky you fine," I mumbled as his uncle walked over to us.

John the Baptist

To the average person, there was nothing going on between Salem and Meya. They were close, like brother and sister because they practically grew up together. But as I watched them interact with each other in the cut of L.O.V.E I knew it was more to it than that between them. That wasn't friendship. That was love. Omen was right – they are each other's weaknesses. To break their kingdom, I had to break their relationship by putting them against each other, or removing one of them out of the picture and letting the other spiral out of control because of their death.

Meya

First, Nasir stopped by the liquor store. I didn't get out. I was still trying to shake these feelings that were consuming me. When he came out with two bags, he stopped by my car and told me to go home and pack a bag and meet him at the Peabody hotel. He had to have money to drop damn near two stacks on a presidential suite for one night. When we made it into the bedroom I finally took the time to look at him, and he was the second finest nigga I'd ever seen – under Salem.

His brown skin was the shade of milk chocolate. The hair on his face and head was nappy and thick, and I loved that shit. I couldn't wait to grab at his golden topped mohawk and that thick beard made him look so tough and rugged. Not every man looked right with a beard, or should wear one... but Nasir wore his well.

His lips were brown and I could tell he'd been a weed and blunt smoker since his younger days. He was tall in stature, and buff in physique. What intrigued me the most were his tattoos. His arms and the top of his chest were covered with them. I found myself staring at him and licking my lips in desire.

"You staying with me for the weekend," he said as he pulled his shirts over his head.

It sounded like he was telling me. Not asking me. I was about to check his ass for it, but his tattoos caught my attention. *Damn.* This nigga was sexy as hell.

"You must not know who I am?" I asked as he stepped towards me.

He towered over me so I had to look up at him.

"Yea I know who you are. I know who your father is."

"You must be crazy to be talking to me the way you have been then."

He laughed softly and blessed me with that smile again as he covered my cheek with his hand.

"I might be a little crazy, but I'm a man. It don't matter who you are in the streets or who your father is. At the end of the day, you're a woman, and you have to be handled as such. The niggas around you don't have your respect because they submit to your power and let you lead them, but I'm the man, so you will submit to me. I'll give you whatever your heart desires in exchange, but you will submit to me."

"I don't submit to nobody but God and my pops."

He laughed again and went over to the bag he brought in. He pulled out two boxes and handed one to me. I looked at it and smiled. It was a home STD and HIV test.

"Go take care of your business," he said sitting on the bed and taking off his pants.

"What makes you think I planned on having sex with you? You can eat the pussy, but that's it."

"You reserving your body and pieces of your heart for that nigga?"

"What you want my heart for?"

"Shit, you need to be glad a nigga tryna take care of it for you. I hate to see women giving themselves to men who don't value and appreciate them. That shit fucks with me because I was raised to value and respect women. So when I saw you with him, I just wanted to be your heart's protector. Ain't no way in hell I'm gone do that and not see what that pussy feels like. We don't have to have sex tonight, but you not having sex with nobody else but me from this point forward. Understood?"

I couldn't imagine how crazy my face looked. This nigga had me so open and confused I didn't know what to do.

"I don't know anything about you."

"Get to know me, Meya. I'm a street nigga with a heart of gold. I love hard and passionately. I believe in love at first sight and I fall in love fast. I love for a woman to nurture me, so if a woman acts like she cares and she takes care of me, I give her whatever she needs.

I know you're used to being the boss, but with me you gon' have to stand down. I don't want Meya the Boss. I don't want Meya Cedrick's daughter. I want Meya the woman. You're supposed to be my counterpart. You soften me as my woman and let me strengthen you as your man."

*

It was sounding so good. No other man had ever spoken to me like this. There was no way his ass was real. He had to be running game.

"How can I trust what you say?"

"You can't, so let me show you with my actions. I just wanna love you. Don't question my sincerity because you won't believe it until you see it. You're surrounded by frauds in this world on a daily basis. When you're approached by something real it's natural to believe it's fake... but I'm here, and I'm real."

I nodded and walked over to the bed. I sat next to him and prepared to open myself up to a man that wasn't Salem for the first time in my life. Truth of the matter was, I didn't even know how to really be a woman, especially in a relationship. I'd never been in a real relationship with anyone besides Salem, and that shit ended horribly.

"I don't know how to be soft," I admitted.

"It's within you, Love. It's just buried beneath what you felt like you had to be in the position you're in. Being with a real man will draw the real woman out of you." I looked at him and really looked into his eyes. He blushed and lowered them to look at my lips. His hand wrapped around my neck and I bit my lip, hoping his lips were about to cover mine. "Gone take the test, baby, so I can take mine. We can shower, then I can hold ya."

"If you betray me, Nasir, I'm coming for you. Since you know who I am and who my father is you know I'm not playing when I say that. I don't do small talk. My interest isn't captured easily. I'm focused on my money, but if I give you access to my heart... if you somehow make your way inside I know I'm going to fall for you like the earth has no fucking gravity. If you poke holes in my already bruised heart and soul..."

His lips moved closer to mine and I stopped talking, but he didn't kiss me. My face contorted and I couldn't believe I was pouting. *Me.* I was pouting because I wanted this nigga to kiss me. Nasir kissed the side of my mouth and chuckled quietly.

"You still think you not gon' submit to me?" he asked pulling me out of my head.

I smiled and mushed his ass before standing and heading to the bathroom to take the test.

Katara

I'm in love, I'm in love, and I don't care who knows it! Okay, so maybe I'm not in love, but Ricardo got my ass wide open. We talked and vibed all last night and he's cool as hell. He's not a street nigga thankfully, but he's a music producer and videographer so he deals with a lot of them. No ex-wives or crazy baby mama's. He's got his own place and a couple of cars.

He seems pretty cool so far. I agreed to let him take me out again, but he was going to have to meet my pops first. He's a great judge of character and he knows everybody in the streets in Memphis, so if Ricardo is lying to me about anything my pops will be able to find out.

I invited him to the little get together my pops had on a monthly basis. One Sunday out of the month he cooked and we all went over to just kick it and be normal. I didn't know how this one was going to go because of what happened between Meya and Salem last night. I was hoping and praying they squashed that shit before we all got together.

I sent her the picture I took of her and Nasir and told her to check in with me so I would know that she was okay. She called immediately and I smiled as I answered.

"Where you at, Me?"

"Peabody."

"Damn, that nigga took you to the Peabody? He must got some money? Or a credit card with a high limit that he trying to stunt with. What he do? Who is this nigga?"

"How did your night with light skinned go?"

"I'll tell you about it after you answer my questions."

"What were the questions again?"

"He around you?"

"Nah. He went to go and get something to eat. We're staying here until tomorrow night."

"You still coming over tomorrow, right?"

"Yea I'll be there. I don't want to hear your daddy mouth."

"You bringing Nasir?"

"I don't know about all that. Salem more than likely will be there and I don't want them going at it. I actually kind of like this dude. I don't want Salem fucking it up."

I couldn't even respond right away. Did she just say she kind of liked him?

"Y'all fuck?"

"Nah. He made me take a test, so we will eventually, but we didn't last night. We showered and ate and drank and kicked it. He held me and we just talked and got to know each other."

"So, back to my original questions. What does he do and who is this nigga? You want me to run his tags and license?"

"Yea, you can. He's a boxer, so he won't be hard to find. He's got a house here, Vegas, and Miami. He goes back and forth."

"Damn, so if Salem tried to get on his head this might be one nigga that can get up with his ass huh?"

"Hell yea. Them niggas would probably kill each other. I'm not trying to have them nowhere near each other for real. He's a cool nigga, though, I can't lie. His residual income game is amazing. He was telling me how he's never had to use any of the money he makes boxing because of all of the businesses that he's invested in. He has money hitting his bank accounts from business owners all over the States on a daily basis."

"See, that's what I'm talking about. This street money is cool, but we need something that we can do legally and grow old with."

"You know I got us taken care of. I've never told you this because I never wanted anyone to be able to use this against you trying to get to me, but I started us an apartment complex company a year ago. The goal is to have a set of apartment complexes in each state by the time we retire. That's going to take a lot of time and effort, but I know we can do it. We gon' be straight, baby girl."

"When you say we you mean..."

"Me, you, and Say. All of our names are on the license. When we retire we'll be splitting the money three ways. Right now it's in the bank collecting interest."

"Does Salem know?"

"Nope."

"You still mad at him?"

"Nope. To be honest, after my night with Nasir, I don't even care anymore."

"Good. I'm glad somebody was able to pull you away from this crazy ass cycle you're in with Salem."

"We looked so good together on that picture. I can really see myself falling for this nigga, Kat. There's so much potential there. I don't want to fall for the potential and be a fool, but he got me open."

"Trust me, I understand."

"So, you have fun last night with light skinned?"

"Do not start calling him that. His name is Ricardo."

"Ricardo? What kind of black person name is Ricardo?"

"Black people are named Ricardo, Meya. What kind of name is Meya?"

"Eww you must like him. He ain't got no nickname?"

"Doe, country ass. You country as hell, Me."

"Whatever. Ima let you go, though. I'll see you tomorrow. You bringing Doe?"

"Yep."

"Good."

"Aight, boo. See ya tomorrow."

"Bye, love ya."

"Love you too."

Meya

After spending the weekend with Nasir, I went back home feeling like a different woman. It's crazy what care and good energy can do for you. I felt so happy and at peace. I felt wanted and needed. I felt... normal, like a normal woman.

I hadn't been away from him for a full hour yet and my mind was being filled with flashbacks of our nights together. Just the thought of being in his strong arms and his hands stroking every inch of my body had my panties wet – and we didn't even have sex. He'd grip my ass and pull me into him and the pressure of his dick through his boxers had me on the verge of climaxing.

I found myself smiling as I walked around my room. I always had the hardest time trying to find me something to wear and this instance was no different. My uncle Cooper, Katara's pops, was having his monthly get together tonight. While I went from my closet to my bed tossing clothes all on it, my phone sounded off. Because it was Salem's ringtone I didn't answer.

I wasn't mad at him anymore, but I still didn't want to talk to his ass. When my front door opened and closed I sighed and waited for him to walk into my bedroom. I smelled him before I saw him. I turned around and all of the feelings that I thought I threw away for him completely resurfaced.

"I called first this time," he mumbled leaning against the doorframe.

"I appreciate that. Can you knock, though?"

"For what? What could you be doing that I can't see?"

"Say, that's not the point. We need to set some boundaries in this fucked up ass whatever this is we got going. You can't just come over whenever you feel like it and just let yourself in."

"Since when?"

"Since always! I don't do that to you!"

"Where you been? I came over yesterday and you weren't here." My demeanor softened. I turned my back to him and started to go through the clothes on my bed. "You don't hear me?"

He stood behind me and all I wanted him to do was bend me over and come inside.

"Move."

"I can't be near you now?"

"Be near that bitch you was at L.O.V.E with."

"I told you what was up with me and her."

"So!"

He turned me to face him, but I avoided his eyes.

"We back on this you not looking at me shit now, Me?"

"Yea, I guess so."

"Who was that nigga you was with?"

"Why does it matter?"

"Because I need to know."

I let out a hard breath and looked into his eyes.

"Nasir."

"Nasir who?"

"Patterson."

"He in the streets?"

"No."

"What he do?"

"Why does it matter?"

"Pops know about him?"

"Will you stop? You act like I'm marrying the nigga or some shit."

I returned to my clothes and he took a step back.

"You ain't never put another nigga before me, Meya. No other man has *ever* been able to stop you from getting to me. He did. That speaks volumes. Even if you can't see it yet."

I dropped the shirts that were in my hands and shook my head weakly. He was right. Nasir had power over my heart and emotions and no one else had that power, except for Salem. I turned around to face him, but he was gone. I sat on the edge of my bed and fought back tears.

As hurt as I was last night, I would never put that same hurt on Salem. I loved him too much. Even if I didn't want to admit it, there was hurt in his voice, and I caused it.

Katara

I looked around my pop's living room and my heart was full. All of my family and friends were here enjoying each other's company with no drama. My pops and Ricardo met and seemed to have hit it off really well. Now, he and I were chilling in the cut enjoying each other's company. My leg was draped over his lap while he played in my hair. Ricardo and I clicked instantly.

I wasn't sure if this would be a happily ever after ending, but it was definitely a happy right now feeling.

"How long we staying here, Kat? Your folks cool, but I want to spend some alone time with you. I can't even feel on you like I want to out of respect for your father."

I looked over at my pops and smiled.

"We can leave just as soon as Meya gets here. I just want to make sure that she's going to behave and nothing is going to go down between her and Salem."

"Are they always that live?"

"Yep. They don't want to see the other with someone else, but they won't be with each other."

"Why not?"

"It's a long story."

"What about us? Can you see yourself with me?"

My eyes found his and I smiled even harder. If there was anything that my parents taught me, it was that as a woman I was stimulated by what I hear and men by what they see. I learned at an early age not to fall for pretty lies, but to make a man prove that he was worthy of me with his actions.

That kept me from getting my heart broken as much as the average woman because I didn't play around with these niggas. They had to work for me. The frauds wouldn't stick around to put in the work, but the sincere guys would. I'd dealt with one fraud that was able to play me, and I had no interest in bringing that count any higher.

"What do you want from me?"

"Your love. Your loyalty. Your respect. Your body. Your womb. I'm tryna plant some seeds in you, woman."

"You just met me," I blushed as I pulled myself away from him.

"And? Love is a choice. It's a commitment. It's an action. If I choose to love you I'm gon' love you come what may."

"That sounds good, but I gotta see this love in action before I commit to something like that."

"As you should. That just made me want you even more. When you say we leaving?"

"When Meya gets here, crazy."

He nodded and looked towards the door like he could wish her here. I chuckled and kissed his cheek before standing.

"I'll be back. I'm going to see if Say has talked to her."

"Cool."

I walked over to Salem and before I could even ask him about Meya he was questioning me about Doe.

"You rocking with light skinned niggas now?" he teased.

"You and Me gone leave my baby alone. Have you talked to her lately?"

"I stopped by her spot a couple of hours ago." His voice softened and his eyes lowered at the mention of her name.

"She say she was coming?"

"I'm sure she is. She was going through her clothes, so I guess so."

"Y'all cool?"

"If you blessing that nigga with your presence he must not be a standard nigga. Is he worth you?"

"Don't avoid my question, and yes, he is. I can handle myself, Say."

He nodded and put his hands in his pockets.

"I'm here if you need me."

"Salem!"

"We cool. Ain't no friction between us."

"So I can leave and not have to worry about y'all getting into it?"

"You can go and enjoy your man, Kat. You don't have to play referee."

I looked at him skeptically but nodded.

"Aight, call me if you need me."

"You do the same."

I went back over to Ricardo and stood in front of him.

"You ready to go?" I asked.

"Hell yea."

He stood and wrapped his arms around me.

"You sure you don't want to wait for your girl?"

"Nah, she gone be alright. Salem seems to be in a mellow mood."

He nodded and looked towards Salem.

"Cool, lets head out then."

We went over to my Pops and said goodbye and then headed out.

John the Baptist

I watched as Salem shopped for a ring. I wondered if it could have been for Meya. I'd been watching them for the past few days, and they weren't spending as much time together as I thought they would. Either I was wrong, or they were going through some things and this ring was going to be his way of making up for whatever was the problem.

Meya

I didn't go to uncle Cooper's get together last night. I didn't want to be around Salem. Not after our exchange. I spent the night talking to Nasir on the phone. I woke up this morning to his Facetime request.

He told me to be ready to go at five this evening and to be dressed casually. I dressed in overall shorts and a white crop top. My hair was flat ironed bone straight with a part down the middle and I had on my signature red lip stain. I nervously waited for him to arrive. I can't lie, I was falling for him hard.

To make sure my mind was clear for Nasir, I called Salem to check on the business and to see if he'd heard anything else about this John the Baptist nigga. He answered after the first ring as he always does.

"What's up, Me?"

"Anything going on with John the Baptist?"

He was silent for a few seconds before he sighed into the phone.

"Nah. Nobody knows anything. Nobody has heard anything. You wanna shut down a few spots just in case he tries to hit us?"

"What you think?"

"I don't think it's necessary at this point. We can afford to take a hit if he tries anything, but I don't want to lose any money trying to avoid something that might not even happen."

"I agree. He's probably not going to make a move any time soon because we're expecting him. Did y'all beef up the cameras and security at the warehouse? That's my main priority."

"Yea. And the houses. We good. I got somebody watching you too."

"Say, you know I don't need all of that."

"I know, but I can be at peace knowing you're good when I'm not around. They'll never approach you unless something suspicious is going on around you."

I smiled softly and sat deeper in the couch.

"Thanks," I mumbled.

"You know I love you, Me, right?"

"Not right now, Salem."

"Then when? I can't tell you I love you no more? You must really like this nigga. I need to meet him."

"No," I said quicker than I wanted to. "All that ain't necessary."

"What you doing tonight?"

"I'm going out. I didn't call you for all this, Salem. I called you to see about the business. Nothing personal."

"Why you got such a fucking attitude, mane?"

"Because you fucked me and was with another bitch the next damn day!" I yelled standing.

"You still on that shit, Meya? I told you what was up with that."

"Did you fuck her?"

"I told you I didn't."

"I hate you, Salem. You know that? I really do hate you."

"I know, baby. I'm sorry."

Nasir knocked on my door and I damn near jumped out of my skin.

"I gotta go."

"You going out with that nigga?"

"Yes."

"Be careful, Me. I'll be at your spot at midnight. That's your curfew. If you ain't home by then, I'm sending them boys after you."

"Nigga, I am not a child. I don't have no damn curfew. You can gone on with that bullshit."

"Aight, play with me if you want to."

He hung up in my face and I cursed myself for calling his petty ass. My mood was pissy as hell, but I opened the door and set my eyes on Nasir and all of that changed. He pulled me into his arms and gave me the deepest, warmest hug I'd ever gotten in my life.

It was like he knew I needed that shit. His hands slowly made their way to my face and I moaned involuntarily as his lips found their way to my neck. When he released me I felt like I released all of that negative energy and was a new woman – his woman.

"Hey, Beautiful," he spoke.

"Hey, Handsome. Let me grab my purse and lock the door and I'll be ready to go."

"You don't need your purse. All you need is your license and your keys. You can leave everything else here."

"So that means you're giving me your undivided attention and you won't be in your phone?"

"Absolutely. I wouldn't ask anything of you that I wasn't willing to do myself."

My smile grew as I stepped back into my house to grab my license and keys. After locking up he grabbed my hand and led me to his car.

"Where you taking me?" I asked as he opened the passenger door for me.

"Picnic and some jazz."

"That's different. I wasn't expecting that from you."

"That's why we're doing it."

He closed my door and made his way to the driver's side and I reached over to open his door.

"Thank you, baby," he mumbled as he got in.

Baby. My mind instantly went back to Salem. I didn't know how I was going to pull this shit off.

∞

After our picnic and live jazz session he took me back to his home. It was a beautiful four bed three bath home in Germantown. His master bathroom was literally the size of my bedroom. What fascinated me most, though, was the bedroom that he'd turned into a reading room. Most people didn't know this about me because they weren't close enough, but I loved reading.

When I was younger I begged my pops to let me learn his hustle. The only way he allowed me to learn was if I stimulated my brain by reading and paying attention in school and bringing home nothing but good grades. We drank only half of our bottle of Port, so we went into his reading room and he made a little pallet for us on the floor. Then Nasir poured us a glass and we just... talked.

I was not expecting this shit from this nigga. He looks so rough and so hood. He talks so rough and so hood. But he has this other side of him that's so loving and gentle and he's so deep and intelligent.

"What's your greatest strength?" he asked.

"I'm not afraid. My pops raised me to be strong and confident and to have no fear. I can't think of one thing that I've ever been afraid of. What about you?"

"My loyalty. Sometimes I'm too loyal to the wrong people for too long."

"I've never had that problem. Well, once, but... that situation has always been complicated."

"What situation?"

"I... don't really want to talk about that with you."

"It's a nigga?"

I nodded and took a gulp of my wine.

"Tell me about this nigga that you've been too loyal to."

"Nasir, I really don't want to talk about that. It's just... I... have been waiting for him..."

"*Had* been waiting for him."

That one simple word along with the sound of his voice damn near made me lose my train of thought.

"Had been waiting for him, when all he's done is make it clear that he doesn't want to be with me."

"The dude from L.O.V.E.?"

"Yea. He's like a brother to me and he doesn't want to take our relationship there out of respect for my father and I can respect that... he's just... the only man I've ever loved besides my father and I'm not used to not getting what I want," I chuckled as tears filled my eyes. "Why am I getting emotional over him when I'm here with you?"

"Because you love him."

I sighed as he wiped a tear from my cheek. A tear that I didn't even realize had fallen. Instead of removing his hand from my face he stroked my cheek with his thumb and stared into my eyes. He looked into my eyes like he could look straight through me and into my soul.

He looked into my eyes with so much care in his, my heartbeats literally slowed down – trying to get the most out of this moment with him.

"I don't want to love him anymore," I confessed weakly. "Make me love you," I pleaded.

"Meya, I don't want you to confuse your love for me with your pain because of him."

"I won't."

He looked at me like he didn't believe me and I didn't blame him. I wouldn't have believed me either.

"I tell you what... I'll love on you and give you what you want and need, and if you are wise and open enough to see what you have in me that's cool, but I don't want to rush this love thang because I want it to last. Now I can fuck that nigga out of you. I can fuck you so good the sight of him reminds you of how much you want me."

My pussy throbbed. I closed my eyes and tried to compose myself.

"Do that." I heard that shit fall from my lips, but I couldn't believe I'd actually said it.

His hand went from my face to my waist as he pulled me on top of him. The doorbell rang and we both looked at each other with confused looks on our faces. I stood and he did the same.

"Stay here," he ordered leaving the room.

Like I was the average chick. He opened the door and I heard muffled voices until he yelled my name. I rushed down the stairs and saw two of my workers on the other side of the door.

"You have got to be fucking kidding me," I said as I walked towards them. "The hell are y'all doing here?"

"Salem said to bring you home."

I chuckled angrily and ran my fingers through my hair.

"Fuck Salem. Tell him I said that."

"Um, he's on the phone. He said if you don't leave with us he's going to come and get you."

"Let um come then," Nasir said.

"No. That's... no. I'll go. Y'all go to the car I'll be out in a few seconds."

They nodded and walked away as Nasir turned around to face me.

"You ain't going nowhere, Meya. Let that nigga come over here if he wants to."

"Nasir, please. He's very protective and possessive of me because he promised my pops that he would watch out for me. He's only acting like this because he doesn't know you," I reasoned.

"Nah, that nigga doing this because he doesn't want anyone else to have you. I want you, but I'm not sharing you and I'm not playing these games. Get your shit straight with him and then find me."

"Find you? Nasir..."

"Nah, Meya. Get your shit straight with him and then find me."

"Fine!" I yelled, angrier with me than him. I tried to walk off, but his hand around my forearm stopped me. He pulled me into him and looked down at me.

"Who you yelling at?"

"You. You're practically dismissing me and telling me you're done fucking with me after I just told you that I didn't want to have shit to do with this nigga."

"You saying that means nothing to me. Do something about it. Cut his ass off. Then I'm all yours."

I looked into his eyes for a few seconds more before nodding and leaving. Salem's ass was about to get it.

∞

When I walked into my house and saw Salem sitting on the couch watching TV, all calm and shit, I was ready to snap on his ass, but I laughed instead and slowly made my way to him. He looked at me briefly before returning his attention back to the TV.

"Thought I told you to be back at midnight?"

"Are you fucking serious right now, Salem? I should beat your ass for interrupting my date. The hell were you thinking sending Marlon and Derrick to get me? Who does that shit?"

"Did you fuck him?"

"No."

"Did you kiss him?"

"No."

"Come here."

"No, Salem. I'm home, so you can go. Go lay up under that bitch you was at L.O.V.E with."

"Really, Meya? We gone talk about this every time we talk?"

"If you leave we won't have to."

"You don't want me to leave."

"I want you to stop playing with me."

"How am I playing with you?"

"Are you crazy? You think this is normal?"

He let out a hard breath and shook his head.

"Come here, Meya."

"No. I'm tired of this, Say. You don't want me. You've made it clear that you don't want me. I'm not going to keep playing with you. I'm not going to let you ruin this for me. Nasir is a good man and he wants me, unlike you. Let me go. If you care about me at all let me be loved by him."

"That's how you really feel?" he asked standing. He stood in front of me and I avoided his eyes as usual. "Look at me," he commanded.

I shook my head no and tried to step back, but he grabbed me by my overalls and pulled me into his chest.

"Look at me, Meya."

"Just go, Salem, please."

"Look me in my eyes and say that shit. Tell me you want me to let you go and I'm done."

His hand gripped my chin and he lifted my face.

"I…" I closed my eyes as the conversation I had just had with Nasir replayed in my mind. "I want you to let me go."

"Fuck that! I ain't never letting you go."

"Salem!" I pushed him and he just laughed like the crazy ass nigga he is.

"Fuck that, Me. This shit for life. The sooner you get that through your head the better off we'll be."

"No, fuck *that*. I'm not gon' be single for the rest of my life playing with you, Salem. I'm done."

"You done?"

"I'm done. I don't want you no more. You wanted us to be brother and sister, right? So, let's be that. Let me take this chance at love and normality, Salem, please."

"Okay, Me. I'll give you what you want." His voice lowered as he grabbed my hand and pulled me into him. "I love you."

He kissed my forehead and leaned against my wall.

"I love you too, Salem."

"You know if I could we'd be married by now, right?"

I was so tired of crying over this nigga I didn't know what to do. I nodded and brushed tears from my eyes.

"I love you, baby," he continued.

"I love you too. Go, Salem. I don't know how much more I can take."

"Okay, okay."

He stood up straight and pulled me into his arms.

"If he hurts you… I'll kill him."

I chuckled and held him tighter.

"I know, but I can take care of myself, Say."

"I know you can, but that's my job, Me."

"You have to stand down. You have to give him a chance to be that for me. How can he prove himself if he doesn't have the chance?"

"So you want me to just trust this nigga with you?"

"I want you to trust me. Trust all that you and pops have taught me. I'm going to be fine."

The words hadn't left my mouth completely before his lips were covering mine. I pulled him closer and pushed him away at the same time.

"Go, Salem."

"Okay, I'm sorry."

He walked away, and I couldn't even find the strength to watch him. I just slid down my wall and sat there for the rest of the night.

Katara

Ricardo had taken me to this smooth spot off Highland. It was a hookah lounge and bar and the vibe was super laidback and chill. We were enjoying the atmosphere and each other's company like we had been for the past couple of weeks when he asked me to see if I could get Meya to make a guest appearance in one of his upcoming videos. He said that the nigga that he was recording was a well-known rapper here in Memphis, but he wanted more exposure.

Apparently, he had a rep as being a street nigga, so he wanted her to make an appearance to validate him. If I know my cousin like I think I do, she wouldn't want to have any parts of this, but I told him that I would ask her anyway.

When we were done talking about business and what it would cost to have her come on as a feature if she agreed, he completely flipped the script on me.

"I want you to meet my parents, Kat."

I didn't want to seem like a hypocrite because I made him meet my parents, but... I didn't want to meet his. That meant that this relationship was moving faster than I wanted it to. Meeting the parents meant this shit was getting serious. Yes, I wanted this... but it was something totally different when you had it sitting in front of you. Like, I wanted love and companionship... but the fear of being hurt had me holding back.

"You want me to meet your parents? Why?"

"Because I like you and I want to make sure they like you too."

"Why?"

"Because I want to commit to you."

"Why?"

"Because I like you."

"Why?"

"Katara... what the hell, mane?"

"I'm sorry. It's just... that's a big step for me. That means this is getting serious."

"Is that a problem? I thought that was what you wanted?"

"It's not. It is. It's just..."

"Do you trust me?"

I covered his hand with mine as my eyes watered.

"Of course I do."

"Then what's the problem? You think I'm gon' do you wrong?"

"No. I mean… I don't think you will intentionally. You're like a Christmas gift for me. I've wanted you for so long and now that I have you I don't want to open you and experience you. I just want to put you on my mantle and admire you to keep from breaking you or finding out that you're not as good as I thought you'd be."

He took a pull of our hookah and sat deeper in his seat.

"So, what you saying, Kat? Do you just need more time for now, or is this how it's always gonna be? Am I gonna always have to prove my loyalty towards you because you don't want to be hurt or disappointed? You so scared of losing me that you don't want to fully have me?"

"It sounds crazy when you say it," I mumbled.

He chuckled and sat closer to me.

"You want me?"

"You know I do."

"Then have me. I ain't going nowhere, baby. I ain't the best nigga in the world, but I'll do whatever it takes to keep you satisfied. Give me you. I'll do right by you." I clutched my heart and shook my head, trying to shake my doubts out. "I'll pull down the stars for you, girl, but I can't force you to take them hoes."

I chuckled, pulled his face to mine, and he kissed my lips sweetly. He parted my lips with his tongue and sucked the top one. At that moment, any fears I had seemed to slip away. I didn't know what the future held for us, and I was okay with that. I had a horrible habit of over thinking and over analyzing situations because I felt like if I was prepared for all possible outcomes the bad ones wouldn't hurt as bad. With Ricardo, I didn't care if we lasted a year or a hundred, as good as he made me feel, every day felt like eternity in heaven and I was going to take full advantage of each one.

∞

Ricardo and I went to Sprouts to grab a pack of pulled beef that had already been seasoned with Korean BBQ seasoning, bell peppers, and onions. I was going to fix that with some white rice, Mexican corn, and a spinach salad. It was damn near ten o'clock and his high had him horny and hungry. I could help with the hunger... that other craving... not so much.

He was cool, though. He didn't sweat me for my sex. He took the time to get to know me and just... spend time with me. The sexual tension between us was thick, but it never over powered the genuine connection we shared.

His arms wrapped around me and I felt his dick at the bottom of my back. I couldn't help but let out a quiet moan as I squeezed his thighs from behind.

"Kat?"

I lifted my head and looked into Pete's eyes. Of all the people I had to run into... it had to be Pete. The rapper who was so deep in Meya that he blew my phone up for days on end trying to get to her.

Ricardo went from behind me to in front of me at the sound of Pete's voice. I looked up at him and ran my hand down his back softly.

"He ain't for me. He for Meya," I informed him quickly.

He looked down at me and nodded as he stepped to the side of me and leaned against our basket.

"What's up, Pete?" I asked as he took a step towards us.

"Where your cousin at?"

"I don't know. I don't keep tabs on her like that."

"You used to. Couldn't see one without seeing the other."

"Well... I don't know where she is, Pete."

"Tell her I'm looking for her."

"Still?"

"Yea, still."

His voice was a little firmer and louder than Ricardo liked because he stepped in front of me again.

"Aye, watch how you talk to her, alright? Lower your voice. Matter fact... just excuse yourself. She don't know where Meya is, so y'all don't have nothing else to talk about."

Pete looked around Ricardo to me as his jaws clenched. He didn't have his entourage with him tonight, so as I expected he bowed down. He took a step back and told me to make sure I tell Meya he's looking for her. I nodded and he walked away.

Ricardo didn't move until Pete was no longer in sight. Then he returned to the back of me like nothing had happened. He wrapped his arms around me again and I looked at him from the side.

"The hell was that?" I asked.

"What?"

"That."

"What?"

"Ricardo…"

"That nigga was annoying me. Tryna get loud and shit like he didn't see me standing here. I can see why your cousin don't want to have nothing to do with him."

I shook my head with a smile and started pushing our basket again. As I tossed the meat into our basket, I made the mental note to tell Meya about Pete. Although I'm sure at this point, with everything she had going on, Pete still wouldn't be able to talk himself into getting even a second of her time.

Meya

Nasir had become my workout partner when I told him about my past with Kendrick. We had finished working out and eating a light lunch when he dropped me off and told me that he was picking me up a little later for our date. A few weeks had passed since I told Salem that I didn't want to have anything to do with him anymore. Surprisingly, he had kept things on a professional level each time we talked.

I was scheduled to meet up with Kat for a spa date, but Salem called me to the warehouse for an emergency meeting. I was hoping it didn't have anything to do with John the Baptist, but since he didn't want to talk about it over the phone I figured it did. Kat scooped me up and we met Salem at the warehouse before we headed to Massage Envy.

When we walked inside of the warehouse and I saw him laughing and joking with a few of his niggas and I smiled inadvertently. It didn't matter what we were going through, he was still a beautiful man to me. He looked our way and his smile faded. I lowered my eyes and inhaled deeply. I made my way over to him as I bit both of my lips and prayed this shit didn't turn into a scene. We had been doing good by each other. I wanted it to remain that way.

"What's up, Kat? Me?"

She nodded and hugged him before walking away.

"What's up?" I asked.

"John the Baptist made his first move."

I sighed heavily and took a step back.

"What was it?"

"He took our biggest suppliers. Omar and Rodriguez don't want to have anything to do with us anymore."

"Okay, so we'll just have to find someone else, or order more from the Miami connects. I'd prefer to work with them anyway."

"And how long you think that's gon' last, Me? Them niggas won't want to jeopardize their own businesses just to keep ours when they find out that he's after us. They gon' fold just like Omar and Rodriguez did."

"What do we need to do then?"

"I talked to pops this morning. We have two options. We can start cooking and growing it ourselves, or we can go directly to Mexico City and get the shit ourselves."

"No. That's too risky. Both of those are too risky. We can't get caught cooking that shit. It's bad enough that we have the shit in this warehouse. I don't want our hands to have to start touching it. How would we even get there and back with it? That's too risky."

"Then what do you suggest we do?"

"Track this nigga down and dead his ass or offer him more than what whoever is paying him to smoke us out is. My father's business has done well for my entire life because he runs it safely and intelligently. He works with suppliers he can trust. If we can trust the Miami niggas…"

I sighed and ran my hands down my face. This was not something I wanted to be dealing with in the middle of my day. I was going to have to get a two-hour massage to try and work this shit out.

"Listen, we can find us some niggas here in Memphis that don't value their lives and freedom, but are loyal as hell to cook the shit and store it for us. For the right price they will die for this shit or go to jail as long as they know they're going to be taken care of. You put five hundred thousand on the table and a nigga will damn near sell his soul to get his hands on it."

"But how will we know we can trust him?"

"Leave it to me. I know a couple of street niggas who have been in and out of jail for their entire lives. It wouldn't be new to them if they ever had to go back."

"But what if he tries to kill them? What nigga would lay down his life for us?"

"He wouldn't be laying it down for us. He would be laying it down for the streets. These niggas live and breathe this shit, Me. Death is a part of the game. Just leave it to me. If you want, we can ride with the Miami niggas and see what happens, but we need to be ready to go to Mexico or start cooking the shit. We can't lay down if he hits us. We can't fold. We have to have a backup plan until we figure out who he is and how to shut him down. Unless you're ready to stand down."

"Hell nah I ain't ready to stand down."

"Then trust me. Trust me, Meya," his hand wrapped around my waist, but he removed it quickly. "Sorry."

"It's fine. I trust you. Whatever you think we need to do I'm down."

"Cool. If this nigga is watching us I don't want him to know that we're working with any new niggas. All communication will be done through burner phones. I'm going to have Marlon and Derrick sweep your house and make sure he hasn't planted any cameras or recorders in there. We're going to let Esau do the pickups and drops for us because no one knows that he works for us. No one from the team is to go to the new warehouse. We cannot afford for him to know that it belongs to us."

I nodded in agreement. It was times like this that I wanted Salem most. I took a step back and reminded myself of the god that I was going to be with a little later tonight.

"I'm wit' it. Just keep me updated. I'm going to switch the accounts out just in case he tries to drain those."

"Smart. Let the rest of your clients know he's in town. Give them the option of leaving or continuing to work with you. The real ones will stay, if they leave we don't need them."

"Cool. I'm going to head out. Me and Kat have a spa appointment."

"Let me walk you out."

His hand covered my forearm and he turned me around. Slowly, we walked outside. When we made it to the car he looked behind us to see if anyone was coming out before he leaned against Katara's car and pulled me into him.

"How you and your nigga doing?"

"Fine, Say. How you and your girl doing?"

He shrugged and blew out a hard breath as he ran his fingers down my arm.

"We doing good. You know how bad I want you right now, right?"

"Trust me I do. I want you just as bad."

He moved his hand to my neck and I closed my eyes in anticipation as I rested my hands on his chest.

"You ready, Me?" Kat asked ruining the moment.

I opened my eyes and pulled myself from his grasp.

"Yea, thanks. I'll um… talk to you later, Salem."

"Can I come over tonight?"

"She has a date," Kat replied getting inside of her car.

"Mane, ain't nobody talking to your blocking ass," Salem said pulling me back into him.

"Fuck you, Say! Get your ass off my car!" she yelled, slamming her door.

I chuckled and pulled him off of her car.

"I have a date tonight... besides..."

"I know I know. We don't need to take it there."

I smiled softly and ran my hands down his chest.

"I love you, Salem."

He tilted his head and put his hands in his pockets.

"I love you too, Me."

"We'll talk later."

He nodded and opened the door for me. When I was inside he leaned in and kissed my temple, then my cheek, and the side of my lips.

"Gone, Salem." Kat ordered. "You get this girl in her feelings I'm gone be the one that has to deal with the shit when she starts acting crazy. Leave her alone now."

He laughed as I turned to face him. We were so close my lips brushed against his naturally. His freaky ass licked them and sucked the shit out of my bottom lip. I moaned and threw my arms around his neck.

"Ima back this car up and swerve yo ass if you don't get out of my car, Salem!" Kat yelled.

"Alright, alright." Salem pulled himself out of the car and stared at me as he closed the door.

"Can I come over tonight?"

I knew I should have no, but my pussy was screaming yes. Nasir and I hadn't even kissed yet and my horn dog ass was about to explode.

"Yea, I'll call you when I get home."

"No, I'll be there when you get back. Midnight, Me."

"Fine."

He walked away and I didn't even want to look at Kat's mean ass. She reversed and I saw her shaking her head out of the corner of my eye.

"You bet not have sex with that nigga, Me. You been doing good. I'd rather you fuck Nasir tonight than Salem. Y'all need to keep the distance y'all have going on. Keep this shit on a business level. Do not fold."

I nodded and took her words into consideration. Salem had a hold on me that no other man had been able to break loose. Nasir was close, but as long as I continued to mess around with Salem even he didn't stand a chance.

Katara

After I dropped Meya off I headed for Ricardo's spot. He told me he wanted to kick it with me tonight and I was so relaxed from my massage and facial I didn't even want to go out. I just wanted to lay around and chill. I called and let him know that I was outside, but before I went in I called Salem. I knew Me wasn't going to turn him down, so I wanted to try and talk some sense into him.

"What's up, Kat?"

"Will you please not go over there and fuck up my cousin's life tonight?"

"I need her, Kat."

"No you don't. If you're not going to do right by her leave her alone. Y'all gone fuck and she gone get in her feelings and start hating your ass. This John the Baptist shit is too important to be getting distracted. If y'all want to go back at it after this is over, I can accept that because I know how y'all are, but please... not right now. Let her do her thang with Nasir. Don't fuck with her head, Say."

"I hear you. I didn't think about it like that."

"I know you didn't. That's why y'all got me."

"You right. I appreciate you. I guess I'll call her and let her know I won't be coming through."

"Cool. She gone be mad at me but I don't care. I'd rather her be mad at me than you. She can't function right when she be going through shit with you."

He chuckled and I smiled.

"Where your crazy ass at, mane?"

"Ricardo's house."

"That nigga treating you right?"

"You know I wouldn't have it any other way."

"That's what I like to hear. I'll get up with you later, though. Ima call your cousin and let her curse me out for playing with her emotions."

"Cool. I love you, and I only want what's best for y'all."

"And we appreciate that. I love you too, baby girl. Enjoy your night."

"You too."

I disconnected the call and headed for my man's door. I opened it and walked inside and was blessed with the surprise of my life. Ricardo was nowhere to be found, but there were balloons all down his entry hallway with little notes hanging off of them. I picked the first one up and snatched the note off which read – "Because you're beautiful."

Tears immediately filled my eyes as I walked towards the second one and picked that one up. "Because of your smile." Ten balloons later I made it to his bedroom, which was filled with like twenty more. He had the lights dimmed low, and candles were illuminating the room. He stepped out of his bathroom and smiled.

"What's this, Ricardo?"

"Reasons why I can't get enough of your sexy ass."

I cried and laughed at the same time as he made his way to me.

"You the one, Katara. I just… wanted to do something special for you."

No words were forming in my mind to express how special he made me feel. His hands covered my face and he covered my lips with his, but he quickly pushed me away. He removed his clothing piece by piece and I watched him attentively. His body was muscular and his skin was smooth. When he was done he pulled me into him and undressed me.

Was now the time for me to tell him that I was a virgin?

I figured he would figure it out as he picked me up and carried me over to his bed. He laid me down and kissed me deeply. His tongue went into my mouth as his hand found its way to my pussy. He ran his fingers up and down my opening, then stopped abruptly and looked at me. I covered my face in shame.

"Baby… I can't even feel you. Has it been that long… or are you… you're… a virgin?"

He pulled my hands down and forced me to look at him. I nodded and closed my eyes.

"Why didn't you tell me? I don't want to rush you."

"I want you to be my first. I trust you with me."

"Are you sure?"

"I'm positive, baby. Open me up."

He moved down to the treasure between my thighs and pushed them apart widely. Ricardo stared at my pussy for a few seconds before licking it, sucking it, and pulling a moan from me that I'd never heard escape my mouth before. He took so much care with my pussy that it literally brought tears to my eyes.

Slowly, he slid his middle finger inside of me and began to push it in and out. Heat radiated from my body as he sucked on my clit and massaged my insides at the same time. I got even wetter. My moans got even louder. And before I knew it my walls and my legs were shaking as I experienced my first orgasm. He lifted himself from me and kissed me, allowing me to see for myself what I tasted like.

I wrapped my legs around his waist while he ran the tip of his dick up and down my clit.

"Are you sure?" he asked again before licking and sucking my neck with the same pressure that he'd just assaulted my clit with.

"Yes, baby. I'm ready."

His eyes found mine, and he slowly pushed himself inside of me.

"Fuck," he muttered pulling back out.

"Wh- what's wrong?"

"You gone be tight as hell and I'm not gonna want to pull out."

Ricardo stood and walked over to his dresser. After pulling a condom from the top drawer he opened it and returned to me. He put the condom on the side of us and ran his fingers up and down my pussy lips.

"I want to feel you first, but Ima put this on, okay? Just let me make you cum first."

"I don't care, Ricardo, just get inside of me."

He did. Slowly. So slow it felt like it was going to take him forever to break through. He was so long. So thick. The shit was hurting bad as hell, but whenever it felt like he'd gotten an inch in he would pull it back out, wetting it, and making it even easier for him to come through. By the time he made his way inside of me completely I was shuddering, clawing up his back, and moaning like crazy.

"Tell me if you want me to stop." His voice was so low, so sincere, so lustful.

He stroked me so slow and deep I couldn't even breathe. Tears fell from my eyes, but I refused to ask him to stop. My pussy started smacking and clamping down on him tighter and tighter. I pulled him down to me and kissed him as long as I could before my moans consumed me. He buried his head in my neck and moaned himself as my pussy began to throb so hard it felt like it had a heartbeat.

My legs fell weakly from my second orgasm. Ricardo pulled out and put the condom on as he said he would. I couldn't help but smile and feel myself falling for him even more. He got on his knees and grabbed my legs by my thighs.

Looking down at me, he bit his lip and closed his eyes as he rubbed my clit with his thumb.

"Are you okay?" he asked as he pulled my ass up on his thighs and slid right back inside of me.

"Yes, please don't stop," I moaned breathlessly.

"That dick feel good?"

His strokes sped up and my lips opened in pleasure. I nodded as I moaned yet again and found the strength in my legs to open them wider and give him even deeper access to me. He smiled and leaned down against me.

"You feel so good inside of me, Ricardo," I answered finally as I wrapped my arms around his neck.

He lifted me higher off of the bed and pounded into me even harder, but he kept his slow speed, which drove me insane. I hissed and held him even tighter. I bit down on his neck and surrendered to my third orgasm, completely content with the fact that I'd given him the most valuable part of me.

Meya

When Salem called me and told me that he wasn't coming through tonight I didn't even let that shit faze me. I was disappointed at first, but when he explained why I agreed because it made sense. Right now, our main focus together was the business. Us adding anything personal along with it was going to block our vision. We got off the phone peaceably and I prepared for my date with Nasir.

I chose to wear a white sleeveless jacquard dress. In the middle of it there was a design that looked like a splash of paint in multiple colors. I paired it with red pumps and a red clutch and wore my hair in loose beach waves. I didn't have on much makeup. I loved to see my face glow, so I did a light highlight, eyeliner and mascara, and a red lip.

Nasir took me to Restaurant Iris where he reserved a private room for us. We had a five course meal and a bottle of wine, then we headed back to his place. I'd taken a shower in the guest room, while he took one in his room. When I was done I put on one of his shirts and crawled in the middle of his big ass bed and into his arms.

I could have gone right to sleep straight like that, but he'd said something at the restaurant that I wanted him to elaborate on. He told me about the fact that he was raised by his grandparent's and that made him insecure and unsure of himself, and I would have never guessed that he was the insecure type by the way he carried himself.

He had his lights set up to clappers and remotes, so he dimmed the lights low enough for it to not be too bright, but we could still see each other with no problems. When he was done he looked at me and stroked my cheek gently.

"Can I ask you something?" I asked.

"Anything."

"How did it feel to not have either of your parents? I didn't have my mom, but my pops was around. If I didn't have him I don't know how I would have survived. Just looking at how Salem reacted to losing his parents... that gave you both strength in your adult lives, but how were you able to handle that as a child?"

He smiled softly and ran his thumb over my lips.

"I couldn't handle it at first. I couldn't understand why they didn't want me. It wasn't that they didn't want me... they just didn't know how to take care of me. My grandparents were struggling to raise me and they were old school so I wasn't able to wear the latest trends and shit or go out to parties with my friends.

That's what made me insecure. Then I had to watch friends grow up with both of their parents and I couldn't understand why I didn't deserve that. I started to get angry, and that's when I started fighting. Thankfully, one of my old coaches caught me before I got too heavy into fighting and turned to the streets.

He got me in the gym and in a boxing ring and that was that. He started teaching me and being a father to me and helping me get my head on straight. My grandfather taught me how to provide and be a man, but Coach... he taught me how to be a King."

"They all did a great job. You're a great man, Nasir. That's why you love for a woman to nurture you and cater to you?"

He blushed and nuzzled his head between my breasts before answering me. I ran my hand down the back of his head and neck and kissed his forehead as he lifted his head to look at me.

"Exactly. I never had that relationship with my mother, so I cling to women who have that type of energy. I want a family more than anything in this world because I didn't have one growing up. Because I've lost so much, I ain't tryna take no more losses. That's why I'm so tight with you. I'm not trying to give myself to you and you fuck me over, Meya. All my life I've dealt with feeling unloved and unwanted. I'm not trying to deal with that with you..."

I covered his lips with my pointer finger to silence him. I looked from his eyes to his lips as I removed my finger. At that moment, I wanted to guard him and protect him from having to experience hurt ever again. I cupped his cheeks with my hands as he ran his fingers through my hair. Slowly, his face lowered, and as I watched his lips my eyes dropped until they were closed. His lips were on mine for the first time. His grip on my hair tightened as he deepened our kiss.

Nasir's tongue inside of my mouth had my pussy soaking wet. He circled his tongue around mine as he wrapped my right leg around his waist. Biting down on my bottom lip, he ran his fingers down my thigh and over my clit. My back arched involuntarily as he licked and bit my neck.

"Take this shit off," he ordered in a low and husky voice as he pulled on the shirt I was wearing.

I pulled it over my head and watched him lick his way down my stomach to my pussy. He kissed my clit and bit his lip. Fuck it. That made me his. His lips covered my clit and he sucked it as he looked up at me. My legs began to tremble immediately as I moaned in pleasure.

They said that there were at least eight thousand nerve endings in a woman's clit and I swear his ass was putting pressure on each and every fucking one. He ran his tongue from my opening to my clit and just the sight of my cream on his beard and lips had me getting even wetter. Latching on to my clit, he sucked and ran his tongue up and down it and had me coming harder than I ever had before. I cried out and pushed him away, but he gripped my thighs and covered my clit again.

"Please, please, please..." I begged pushing him away.

He chuckled and looked up at me.

"What?" Nasir asked running him thumb up and down my clit.

His beard grazed my thigh and I was bucking again.

"I can't take no more," I admitted pulling him up to me.

His beard brushed against my face and I shivered as I grabbed two handfuls of his hair and looked into his eyes. He began his dive inside of me and I pulled his hair even harder as he filled me.

"Shit," he moaned as he reached the pit of me. Swear it felt like I felt him in my ribs.

I released his hair and clutched his waist, squeezing it and scratching as he dug into me nice and slow. Nasir dug into me so deep it felt like he was hollowing me out and removing every other man that had ever been inside of me. With fingers, tongues, or Salem's dick... I was forgetting all that shit as he stroked me.

He spread my legs wider and brushed against my clit each time he entered me. Between the sound of him smacking against me, my cream pouring out onto him, his heavy breathing, and my moans... my eyes were rolling into the back of my head and I was coming yet again.

I grunted and dug my nails into his forearms as my pussy clenched him even tighter.

"Nasir..." I moaned.

His grip around my thighs tightened. His strokes sped up. He moaned and released my legs, covering his mouth with one hand.

"Shit," he moaned again as he pushed his head back.

I pulled his hand down and he looked at me and smiled before leaning down and kissing me. His hands made their way into my hair and he pulled while stroking me slowly. I moaned into his ear, bit down on it and ran my hands up and down his back.

"Meya," he moaned breathlessly.

I'd heard that a person's name is to that person, the sweetest, most important sound in any language... and hearing him moan it inside of my ear proved that to be true. I brought his face to mine and intertwined our tongues. Stroking his just as slow as he was stroking my bottom set of lips. The feel of his pelvis on my clit, him drilling my G-spot with the tip of his dick, it was all becoming too much for me.

I broke our kiss, only because my lips began to quiver, and he covered my nipple with his.

"Why do I feel you all over me?" I asked as I felt that strong sensation to pee. I was about to squirt. I'd never squirted off the dick. I was about to squirt while this nigga was inside of me. "Ohhhh my Goooddd," I moaned as I tried to push him out of me.

The clear liquids erupted from me and he pulled out immediately and watched as I squirted and my body shook.

"Got damn, Meya," he muttered stroking his dick. He entered me again and started hitting me with those same strokes. "This my pussy, Meya. Nobody else gone fit you like I do. Nobody else gone fuck you like I do. Nobody else gone make love to you like I do. This shit is mine. Do you hear me?"

"Yes, Nasir," I answered quickly as he lowered himself and kissed me quick and nasty. His tongue went deep into my mouth as he sped up his strokes. He rolled his dick around in me and my body locked tightly around his. "Ahhh! It's yours and yours alone."

"Say that shit again," he commanded wrapping his hands around my neck.

"It's yours, Nasir. I'm yours." The dick was feeling so good I heard myself saying shit I'd never said or even thought about a nigga before. "God, I wanna have your babies," I moaned raking his chest with my nails. "Don't ever take this dick away from me, Nasir. It feels so fucking good."

"Damn, girl," he moaned as I came again, but this time, he came with me.

After his orgasm subsided he rolled over to his side, and pulled me along with him, so that he was able to remain inside of me.

72

"Did you mean that shit?" Nasir pushed pieces of hair out of my face.

"Mean what?"

"That you want to have my babies."

I smiled and stroked his cheek.

"I guess I did. Not right now of course. I'm on birth control and I don't want to bring a child into this world while I'm in the game, but... I don't know... there's something about you that makes me want to build with you and experience that with you. I don't know if it's because that family unit is something that we both lacked, or if it goes deeper than that, but I do want to explore that option with you."

He pulled me on top of him and I felt him grow inside of me.

"I know you're on birth control, but let's go again and pretend that you're not."

Katara

"Tell me all about it and don't leave out any details!" Meya yelled as soon as she walked inside of my pop's basement.

My mom cooked earlier so we all came through. We were chilling in the basement smoking and listening to music when she came down. I had texted her earlier and told her that I had finally gave up the cookie and she couldn't wait to hear the details. I tried to tell her over the phone, but her crazy ass said she wanted to see my face while I talked about it.

It was no easy task making it to twenty-six as a virgin, but I was committed to saving myself for my husband. Ricardo was just so sweet and loving though, he really appreciates me... and that shit turned me on so much I couldn't resist. She sat her Straw-Ber-Rita down and sat right in front of me. I blushed and took a swig of mine.

"Girl..."

"Can light skinned get it in?"

"What I tell you about calling him that?"

"Can he?"

"Yaasssss, honey! It was amazing! It hurt like hell at first, but he took his time with me and he was so gentle. He went so slow and gave me time to get used to him. I loved it."

"That's great, baby girl. As long as that was what you wanted to do and not something you were forced into."

"No, he offered to stop a few times, but I wanted to do it. There's something about him that I just can't resist. I think he's the one, Me. I know it's soon... but... he just makes me feel so good inside. He makes me feel like I'm the only woman in the world."

"When you're the only woman in *his* world... that's how it should be. I'm so happy for you."

"How did your date with Nasir go?"

This time, she was the one blushing. She opened her mouth and looked away as she shook her head.

"Damn, was it that good?"

"Let me just say, it was so good the nigga had me saying I wanted to have his kids."

"Stop lying! You fucked him?" I yelled louder than I planned on doing.

Salem looked our way and I buried my head in my hands.

"Katara!" She yelled. "Can't tell yo loud mouth ass shit!"

"I'm sorry. I just... got so excited. You *never* let a nigga inside. Never. Besides..."

Salem was at the table and snatching her up by her forearm.

"Say, don't you hurt her!" I yelled grabbing her purse. Ain't no telling what was about to go down with them.

Meya

It was damn near twenty people in that basement, and not one of them tried to help me get out of Salem's grip. He pulled me up the stairs, through the living room, and out the front door before he said anything to me. When we were outside he started pacing in front of me. I crossed my arms over my chest and waited for him to yell at me. There was no point in denying it or trying to hide it anymore.

"You fucked that nigga?"

Salem stopped pacing and stood in front of me. I scratched my ear and tried to look away, but he stepped in front of me again.

"Salem..."

"Did you? Did you fuck that nigga, Meya?"

"Yes."

He took a step back and massaged his temples.

With a weak and trembling voice, he asked, "Why?"

I looked into his eyes and saw something I'd never seen before – pain. They glossed over with tears.

"Salem..." I reached out to him but he pushed my hands away.

"Why would you do that, Meya?"

My eyes flooded with tears at the sight of his. I had to wrap my arms around myself to keep from reaching out to him again.

"I... he... I like him. He's... he likes me. He makes me feel like a woman, Say. He wants me, and he's not afraid to want me. He wants to settle down with me and fucking marry me and have babies with me. We getting old, Salem. I'm twenty-six, nigga. You think I want to be your secret lover for the rest of my life?"

His hand wrapped around my neck and he pulled me into his chest.

"It's one thing to let a nigga eat my pussy. I was cool with that shit because I know you have needs, but you let another nigga come inside of you? You let another nigga come inside of you? Where your heart and soul resides? Where *my* fucking heart and soul resides? I gave you mine in exchange for yours, and you gave that nigga access to me? That's my space! I don't share that shit with no fucking body!"

I covered his hand with mine and pulled at his fingers, but his grip was firm.

"Salem, let me go."

"How could you, Me?"

"I'm sorry. I didn't want you to find out. I didn't think you would care."

"You didn't think I would care? You trying to fight me and shoot my ass because you saw me out with a female, but you think it's okay for you to fuck another nigga? Type of shit is that?"

"I'm sorry, but I'm not going to wait for you forever. Don't you think I deserve better?"

"I thought you loved me?"

"I do. I swear I fucking do. But I want to love somebody who loves me too."

"I do love you. You know I do."

He released me and I rubbed my neck.

"You love me, but you can't love me the way I need to be loved, Salem. Nasir can."

"So you settling for this nigga then?"

"I'm not saying that. I'm just saying… I'm sorry."

He nodded and took a step back.

"You know what's so crazy about this shit?"

"What, Salem?"

"You used to always say you hated me and I could never understand how you could say you loved me and hated me at the same time, but now I do, cause I hate yo ass now too."

"Salem…" He turned around and started walking towards the house. "Salem, don't do me like this." The tears that I had been holding back began to fall as he continued to ignore me.

When he was inside, I went to my car and got in. I figured once Kat saw him walk in without me she would bring me my purse and I could dip. There was no way I could face him after this.

Katara

I felt bad as hell about Meya and Salem. She locked herself inside of her house for days straight, and she wasn't answering any of my phone calls. I called Salem to see if he had tried to reach out to her, but he hadn't, so I decided to stop by her spot on my way to Ricardo's. I wasn't expecting her to answer, but I at least had to try.

When I made it to her house, I knocked and rang the doorbell and of course she didn't answer. After a few minutes passed I used my key to let myself in.

"Me!" I yelled as I walked down the hall. "I just need to know that you're okay, babe."

I found her laying in the middle of her bedroom floor wearing nothing but a Calvin Klein bralette and boyshort set. There were two empty bottles of Vodka next to her along with three empty Swisher Sweets boxes.

"He won't talk to me," she mumbled.

"Meya..." I walked towards hers and kneeled before her. "Baby, you gotta get up. You can't sulk in this room over that nigga."

"That's easy to say, Kat."

"What about Nasir? I thought you liked him?"

"I did," she whined sitting up.

"Then fuck Salem. Build with Nasir. I get that you love him and you're attached to him, but this is not healthy, Me. Look at you. You've been locked up in here for days. Have you been eating?"

She grabbed a blunt and lit it. After taking a hit she shook her head.

"I ate."

"When?"

She looked at me before turning the other way and blowing the smoke out of her mouth.

"What's today?"

"Are you fucking serious, Me? You talking about you ate and you don't even know what day it is? Get your love sick ass up and eat! And then boss the fuck up! You don't let these niggas knock you off your square. You think that nigga sulking around his crib? Nah. He doing him. Do you, boo. Get up, stack this paper, and make love to that sexy ass man of yours. Fuck Salem."

As if I'd talked him up, Salem called me. I started not to answer but she saw his face on my phone and told me to.

"Yea?" I answered putting him on speaker.

"She answer?"

"I'm here now."

"She good?"

"What you expect, Salem?" He remained silent. "Hello?"

"I'm here. I'm sorry."

Meya stood and snatched my phone.

"Nigga, you didn't see me blowing your phone up? You know I don't like to be ignored. You lucky I didn't come over your house and fuck you and your bitch up."

He sighed heavily into the phone. "Me, give me some time. You hurt me."

"I hurt you? Salem, you've been throwing me to the side for years and I fuck one nigga and I hurt you? Fuck outta here with that bullshit."

She disconnected the call and handed me my phone.

"Kat, you can stay here for as long as you want, but I'm about to take a shower, head by the warehouse to check on this money, and go fuck off with Nasir for a while."

I smiled as I stood.

"I'm gone. My job is done."

John the Baptist

One of the things that made me so great at my job was the fact that there was no information that was off limits to me. When I found out that Salem and Meya were each other's weaknesses I knew exactly how to dismantle the two. Before I went to them directly, I went to Cedrick and offered him the chance to disassemble his organization and make way for my client, but he declined. So, when Salem left his home I left a package for him that was sure to put a wedge between him and Meya.

Now, on to phase two.

Meya

When I made it to Nasir's spot he wasn't even there. I got back in my car and listened to voicemails that he and Katara had left me. The most recent one from him said that he was going to Vegas for a fight and that if I got the message before Sunday night that he could have a ticket waiting at the airport for me so I could join him.

Even though he hadn't heard from me for days straight he wasn't talking crazy, and he still wanted me. I couldn't help but have a heavy heart. Here I was driving myself crazy over Salem when I had Nasir ready and willing to give me all the love I needed. I never even wanted love and a relationship if it wasn't coming from Salem, but Nasir makes me want those things with him.

I rushed home to pack a couple of bags and when I got there Salem's car was in my driveway. I started to just say fuck it and go to Vegas with no personal belongings, but I wanted to hear what this nigga had to say. I walked into my home, unsure of what the hell I was about to walk into.

As usual, his ass was sitting in the middle of my couch, but the TV wasn't on. He was just... sitting there.

"What's up?" I asked walking towards him.

He looked up at me with those empty eyes that I'd begun to hate. I sat next to him and turned to the side slightly to look at him.

"I'm gon' ask you this one time, Meya, and I want you to tell me the truth."

He pulled his gun from his waist and put it on my coffee table. This went beyond fucking another nigga. I held my purse tighter just in case I had to reach for mine. I didn't know what was going on with this crazy ass nigga, but when guns came in the picture it was always every man and woman for themselves.

"Did you know my parents?"

My shoulders relaxed a little, but I was still just as confused.

"What? No. Why?"

"Did you know that my father worked for your father?"

"No, how did you find that out?"

"That's not important. So, you mean to tell me that you didn't know that your father had my parents murdered because he thought my pops was an informant?"

I chuckled lightly from nervousness as I rubbed my suddenly sweaty palms down my pants.

"That's bullshit, Say. Pops wasn't responsible for that. He doesn't even condone killing women."

"Well obviously he made an exception."

"You sound crazy as hell right now, Salem. Where is this coming from?"

He pulled a few crumbled pieces of paper from his pocket and handed them to me. I looked over the police records where it had Salem's father listed as a witness in the murder investigation of Ricky Sanders. The suspect – my father.

"They had no case without my father, so your father had him killed. He didn't know my mother was there, so she had to be killed too."

"Salem… no… there… there has to be an explanation for this. This has to be just a coincidence."

"That's why he took me in, Meya. Not because he had this big ass heart, but because his grimy ass killed my parents and he felt bad about the shit. Maybe he felt bad, or maybe he wanted to keep me close to make sure I never found out."

"This doesn't make any sense. Just because your pops was a snitch doesn't mean my pops killed him."

"I've devoted my life to him, Me… and he hides this shit from me? You know how stupid I feel right now?"

I didn't even know what to say. Could my pops have done this shit? It would explain why he took in a total stranger. No, this couldn't be true.

"Listen, just talk to him. Ask him if it's true before you go to assuming shit."

"Ask him if it's true? Meya, it's right there in fucking black and white! The nigga killed my parents because he didn't want to go to jail!"

I shook my head in disbelief.

"How did you find out? This has to be a mistake."

"Open your eyes, baby. Your father is a murderer. He's not this street nigga with a heart of gold. He's a ruthless street nigga. He did this shit, and he gon' pay for it."

He stood and grabbed his gun.

"Wait, what do you mean he's going to pay for it?" I stood.

"Just what the fuck I said. You think I'm gon' let this shit slide?"

"You don't even know if it's true. My pops has been nothing but good to your ungrateful ass. After all he's done for you you're going to turn on him like this? He probably didn't even know anything about you when... if... he did this."

"Fuck that. He knew. I can't let this slide, Me."

"Salem, just talk to him, please. There has to be more to this than that, but if this is true... you know I'm not going to let you come for my pops without doing something about it, right?"

"If someone killed him and you knew who it was you telling me you wouldn't seek revenge?"

"That's different. He's been here for you, Salem."

"Fuck that! That nigga is the reason I don't have my own damn parents to be here for me! If this is true, he's dead, and if you want to stand in the way of that... you can get it too."

"Really, Salem? After everything we've gone through you're threatening me and my father's lives?"

He put his gun back at his waist before kissing my forehead softly.

"Damn right."

I nodded and took a step back.

"If that's what it comes to, I have no choice but to accept and respect that, but trust and believe, I came up under the same training as you. Don't expect either of us to lay down and accept this shit. You come for me or my pops I'm on your ass."

He nodded and licked his lips.

"You know I love you, Me, right?"

"I love you too. No matter what."

He left, and I grabbed my phone and tried to pull all the strings I could to get in touch with my pops.

Katara

I woke up to multiple missed calls from Me. Ricardo and I spent half of the night and morning exploring each other's bodies, and we didn't get to sleep until about five in the morning. I was dead to the world until about one in the afternoon. I called her immediately and she told me to come to the warehouse for an emergency meeting.

When I got there her car was the only one I recognized. The other two that were parked next to hers had never been there before. I walked in and she was talking to two niggas I'd never met. She looked over at me and shook her head. I walked even faster trying to get to her.

"What's going on?" I asked. "Who are they?"

"Your bodyguards."

"What? Bodyguards for what?"

She grabbed my arm and led me away from the men.

"I think John the Baptist slid Salem some information. It looks like pops had Salem's parents killed. Salem is threatening to seek revenge if it's true, and if I stand in the way of that he's coming after me too. I know he's not going to involve you, but if John has started making his moves I need to keep you safe."

"What? Unc did what? That's crazy. I mean I know he was in the streets, but I never thought he was capable of killing someone."

"Shit, look at me and Salem. Where you think we got it from?"

I nodded and crossed my arms over my chest.

"Damn. When is Salem going to talk to uncle Ced? I hope it's not true. Can they put him in protective custody or something?"

"Nah, and even if they could he wouldn't let them. I'm just going to have to stop Salem from going after him."

"And how do you plan on doing that, Meya? Y'all can't go to war over y'all parent's beef."

She sighed and ran her hand down the back of her neck.

"I might not have a choice, Katara. Salem has always said if he ever found out who killed his parents he was going to handle them. I just have to be prepared."

"I'm going to see if I can talk some sense into him."

"Don't waste your breath. Let me introduce you to the two of them before I head out. They'll take turns being with you all day every day, but you won't be able to sense their presence."

I nodded, still in disbelief.

"Meya, I know you feel like you have to go against Salem on this, but please, try and talk to him."

"I tried, Kat. He ain't tryna hear that shit. I'm not begging for my life or my pops. If he wanna play with them pistols we can do that. I knew what I was signing up for when I begged pops to let me get in the game. I just... wasn't expecting it to come from him."

"So, if these are my bodyguards where are yours?"

She chuckled before kissing my cheek and walking back towards them.

"You know that ain't my style," she threw over her shoulder.

I shook my head and walked back over to them. All I could do was pray that Marlon and Derrick were still watching over her and that their loyalty was still to her and not Salem.

Meya

Salem and I were set to visit my pops in two days. We hadn't said anything to each other since he practically threatened to kill us both. I didn't have a choice but to see him today. I had to drop off some money to him for our next reup. It didn't matter what we had going on personally, business always came first.

I was smoking a blunt and talking to Nasir when Salem pulled up. Nasir was still in Vegas, and I can't lie... I wanted to join him there bad as hell, but I couldn't make any moves until I talked to my pops. He understood my business came first, and he didn't press me to come.

"He's here, Nasir. Let me handle this business and I'll call you back."

"Aight. Call me if you need me. I'll see you in a few days. You know you can always come here, though."

"I know. I appreciate that. I wish I could. You bring me such peace."

"Then come to me, Meya. Leave today and I'll have you back in time enough for the sit down with your pops."

Salem stepped out of his car and I rolled my eyes at the sight of him.

"That sounds good."

"I'll book your flight and text you the information. I'm going to send you my address as well, but I should be able to pick you up from the airport."

"Thanks."

I disconnected the call and walked to my trunk. After hitting my blunt one last time I tossed it and opened the trunk. Salem came and stood next to me. He pulled the duffle bag out, closed the trunk, and leaned against it. I did the same and he intertwined his fingers with mine.

"You remember your eighteenth birthday? You wanted me to take you out, but I didn't want to because I was scared of what Ced might think. So, you went out with that nigga you met at the bowling alley."

I smiled at the thought.

"Yea, you came up there and acted a fool. I was so mad at you that night. I was so embarrassed. I already didn't have too many niggas trying to talk to me because of who my pops is, but after you did that shit they really weren't tryna step to me."

"What about when I tried to take Erica to her prom…"

"Mane, I gave you the hardest time about that shit. I was so jealous. I did *not* want you to go."

"Why not, though?"

"Because. You didn't want to take me to mine. I felt like you liked her and you didn't like me. You know I'm possessive. I just… I don't know. That was something special to me and I didn't want you to share that with her. I wanted you to share that with me."

He looked down at me, but I couldn't look up at him.

"That's when you first started to really express that you had feelings for me. I mean… there was something there the first day we met, but that was the first time you really just showed me that I was what you wanted." I nodded and let out a hard breath. "Follow me," he said removing himself from my car.

"Where we going?"

"Just follow me. You trust me still?"

"Why should I? In two days you could be my biggest enemy. In two days one of us might be dead. Why should I trust you, Salem?"

"If you love me like you say you do, trust me. Follow me."

Part of me wanted to follow him and see where this was going to take me. The other part of me wanted to get in my car and go to Nasir. I got inside of my car and still didn't know which direction I was going to take. My pops taught me not to follow my heart because the heart is reckless and it wavers. So, instead of following my heart and going to Nasir, I followed Salem and prayed I wouldn't regret it.

∞

Salem led me to his house. I didn't know what his ass was up to. I sat in my car and typed a message to Nasir letting him know that I was going to have to switch my flight out, but before I could hit send Salem was opening my door. I quickly exited out of our conversation and met Salem's eyes.

"You can leave that and your purse in your trunk. You won't be needing either one of them."

I rolled my eyes and put my phone in my purse.

"What is this about, Salem?" I asked getting out of my car.

"Do you always have to know everything?"

"Hell yea. My life ain't set up for me to be a fan of surprises. I needs to know what's going on around me at all times."

"What you think I'm gon' do, Me?"

"Shit, Ion know, that's why I'm asking."

"Just put your purse in the trunk so we can go."

I did as I was told and followed him to his front door. After he unlocked it he inhaled deeply and opened the door slowly.

"Hold on for a second," he said closing the door in my face.

"Nigga, really!" I yelled kicking his door. "If this ain't some bullshit."

After pacing for I don't know how long he finally opened the door. I side eyed his ass as I stepped inside, but my anger was quickly replaced with surprise, happiness, sadness, love, and lust at the sight before me. His hallway was covered with rose petals and candles. I turned around to face him, and when I did he pulled a bouquet of white roses from behind his back. My eyes watered immediately.

He had never done some shit like this for me before.

"Um... since I didn't get to take you to your prom... I... wanted to do something special for you, you know... to make up for that."

I couldn't even say anything. I just shook my head in disbelief as he lifted my hand and placed the flowers inside. After using his thumb to wipe my tears away, Salem gently grabbed me by my forearm and led me to his bedroom.

"I got a dress and shit in there for you. Take your time getting ready. When you're done come in the living room." I still couldn't say anything. He smiled softly and kissed my forehead. "Gone."

He pushed me towards his room slightly and I looked back at him briefly before walking inside. The first thing my eyes focused in on was the long red lace dress laying across his bed. It was a sleeveless mermaid fit with an open back and thigh high split.

I couldn't front, he had taste if he actually picked it out. Knowing him, though, he had some chick in the store to pick it out for him. I ran my hands down the dress before going to take a quick shower and putting on the blueberry body butter and spray he had laid out for me.

When I got to the makeup and flat iron I knew Katara had to have helped him because he had my favorite Urban Decay Naked palette and there's no way that was a coincidence. I smiled the entire time I did my hair and makeup.

Once I slid on the sleeveless black bra and panty set he had for me, and dress, I put on the six inch pumps that were at the foot of the bed. With those he and I were going to be eye to eye. After looking myself over once more I opened the door and slowly made my way to him.

If you would have told me that I would be here, in his home, at a prom that he put together for me... I would have bet money that you were a lie, but here I was, and I really didn't know how to feel. I wanted to completely embrace this moment, but it saddened me because in just two days our lives were going to be changed drastically.

The clicking of my heels against the floor gained his attention. He stood and faced me and damn near took my breath away. He'd showered and changed and was wearing an all-white tailor made tuxedo. His shirt, pocket square, and shoes were black. I swear a chocolate man in white would be the death of me.

Especially if it was *this* chocolate man.

Salem sauntered over to me and I scratched the back of my neck nervously.

"You look beautiful, Me." His voice was so low and sincere as he looked my body up and down.

"You look beautiful too. I mean, in a manly type of way."

He chuckled and grabbed my hands.

"Are you nervous?"

"Very," I admitted looking at all that he'd done for me.

His living room was decorated with red and white rose petals and candles. On one table he had wine and fruit, and on another he had two sashes and crowns.

He cupped my chin inside of the space between his pointing finger and thumb and pulled my attention back to him.

"You know I love you, Me, right?"

This time when he asked... it sounded so final.

Biting the inside of my cheek, I nodded. I wrapped my arms around his neck and he wrapped his around my waist.

"I appreciate you for doing this, Salem. This means more to me than you'll ever know. Thank you for this. This makes me feel so... wanted."

"Baby, I want you more than you know. I know my actions haven't made that easy to believe, but that's because I've been more loyal to Ced than I have been to you and me. With everything going on now I feel so foolish for that. I just... even if it's for one night... I just want you to know how much I love you."

His hands covered my neck and he massaged it with his thumbs as he looked into my eyes intensely. He looked into my eyes like there was something inside of his that he needed me to see. Like looking into his eyes would give me access to his heart and soul. Or should I say mine. He was right, we exchanged. I gave him mine and he gave me his ten years ago.

Ever since he made it clear that he wouldn't give me what I wanted and needed I've been trying to get mine back, but in this moment... I didn't regret them being in his care.

I watched him bite down on his bottom lip as he looked at mine and my chest rose and fell in anticipation of his kiss. No one kissed me like him. No one kissed me as soft, hard, slow, deep, nasty, and passionately as Salem Myers.

His lips parted partially and I whimpered.

"Why are you taking so long?" I whined.

His half smile made me smile, but it faded immediately.

"You fucked that nigga, Me."

I was so caught off guard by his statement I just looked at his ass. I ran my fingers through my hair and took a step back.

"Okay, so you don't want to kiss me because of that?"

"I want to kiss you. I want to make love to you. But you let that nigga inside of you."

"Fine. I don't want to talk about him, Salem. I just... let's just make the most out of this moment. We don't have to kiss. We don't have to make love. I don't want to argue."

He nodded and ran his hand down his face.

"I'm sorry, Me."

"It's cool."

I said that it was, and I guess it should have been... but that shit hurt my feelings. To know that he took that shit to heart so heavy made me feel horrible. Besides Salem, Nasir was the only other man I'd shared my body with. As good as it was, we didn't connect the way Salem and I connect emotionally, mentally, and spiritually.

Every time I gave myself to Salem I felt like I was getting to know him on every level intimately. It was more than just sex. It was truly how we expressed our love for each other simply because we couldn't any other way.

When I was with Nasir, Salem was a nonfactor. He didn't matter. I felt normal. But when I was with Salem nothing else in the world existed. No one else mattered. I felt whole. I felt like the pieces of me that were missing had been returned... even if for just a moment.

A moment like this.

We walked into the center of his living room and he cut on some music. *Day by Day* by Bobii Lewis came on and we both smiled.

"You know that's what you are to me, right?" He asked flipping through the songs for something slower.

"I know, Salem."

When he made it to Chrisette Michele's *Golden* he stopped. I shook my head adamantly as tears filled my eyes. That was supposed to be our wedding song.

"Salem... no... I can't..."

"Shhh..."

He grabbed me by my hips and pulled me closer. Slowly, we began to sway left to right.

Our hands traveling each other's bodies like we hadn't already written the map. Like he didn't know every spot to touch to make me moan. Like I didn't know every spot to touch to make him groan. Like he hadn't claimed me and left his mark deep within me. Like I wasn't the only woman his dick would get hard for.

His hands cradled my cheeks and I closed my eyes. Too overwhelmed to look into his as tears overflowed from mine.

"Life's not always perfect, but love is always forever," he uttered.

"Be the man of my dreams and get down on one knee love."

"Let's take two golden bands and let's walk down the aisle love."

"I'll say I do and you'll say I do make a golden commitment love."

I hung my head, but he lifted it and kissed my forehead, letting his lips remain briefly. He kissed my eyes. Then my nose. His forehead rested on mine as his hands ran down my arms until they connected with mine. He kissed the side of my lips and they opened against my will.

"I love you," he whispered into my lips before kissing them hard and long.

I collapsed into his body and felt like I literally melted inside of him. Like somehow I was coming out of myself and becoming him. His hands found their way to my ass as he licked my lips and slid his tongue inside of my mouth. I happily accepted and fought the urge to thank him for blessing me with it. From my mouth to my neck to my chest his tongue had me shivering.

I pushed him away and he looked at me like I was crazy.

"If you're not going to make love to me by the end of the night stop playing with my emotions, Say."

"You would open your big ass mouth and ruin the moment," he replied pulling me back into him.

With one hand behind my neck and the other running through my hair, Salem looked into my eyes and I swear he had never looked at me so lovingly before.

"Why are you doing this to me?"

I tried to remove his hands from me, but he wouldn't let me.

"We need this."

He released me finally and walked over to the table that held the wine and fruit. After pouring us both a glass he nodded for me to come to him. I did and we sat down. He handed me the wine and I gulped that shit down immediately. He laughed as he reached for the bottle.

"Are you thirsty?"

"I'm nervous."

"Since when did I start making you nervous? You don't fear anything."

I thought that was true, but I was beginning to become more and more aware of my fear and my weakness – loving and never really having, or even losing him.

"I thought that too," I mumbled before drinking half of my second glass of wine.

"What are you afraid of, Meya?"

"Losing you. I know you were never really mine to have but… Salem you're my best friend. As much as I hate your ass… nigga, I love you. You've been my day one for ten years. What am I going to do if I can't have you? What if my pops really killed your parents? There's no way I can let you go after him, and I can't help but understand if you wanted to go after me…"

"Please. I don't want to think about that right now. Like you said earlier, let's just make the most of this moment. Tonight you don't have to be afraid, because you have me, and nothing or no one is going to stand in the way of that."

I leaned back into the couch and let Al Green sing to me about it raining in his heart. Salem's hand made its way to my thigh as it normally did when we were sitting this close, and I covered his hand with mine.

"What's one thing that you've always wanted to ask or tell me that you never have before?" I asked.

"Shit... one thing I've always wanted to ask you is why you love me."

"Why haven't you asked before?"

"Just didn't seem like a fair conversation to have. Nothing could come of it, and your mean ass be quick to tell a nigga you hate him."

I chuckled and squeezed his hand lightly.

"I don't really hate you, Salem. I just hate our situation. I love you because you're my best friend. You're the only person that I can really be myself with. I can't even really be me with Kat, but with you... you accept me just as I am. You're patient with me. You have no problem showing me selflessness.

You've been here for me and my father tough and as I grew in respect for you my love for you grew as well. It went from wanting to be your friend to wanting to experience you on deeper levels. I've known you as my friend. I've known you as my brother. I've known you as my business partner. I've known you as my rider. I've known you as my lover.

But I'll never get to experience you as my husband. As the father of my children. I don't even know where that came from. That was so off topic."

I removed my hand from his and put a little distance between us.

"That was the one thing you've always wanted to tell me. Now what have you always wanted to ask me?"

"How is it so easy for you to be without me?"

"What makes you think it's been easy?"

I shrugged and scratched my scalp.

"You sure make it look easy."

He stood and held his hand out for me. We walked back to his bedroom in silence. Salem went under his bed and pulled a box out and handed it to me. Then he went into his closet and pulled out an even bigger box.

"What's this?" I asked.

"Open it."

I opened the box and ran my hand through hundreds of pieces of paper. I looked up at him and he came and sat next to me.

"Every night, Meya, this is how I put myself to sleep." I pulled one of the pieces of paper out and sat the box on the ground. I ran my finger across my name on the top of the paper. "Every night, I write to you. I say the things that I can't say to you. I can't hold you, so I write about how much I wish I could. You think this shit is easy for me? I've been in love with you since I was a young nigga. You think I like turning you down? I don't. This shit fucks with me, Me.

When I'm done writing I put the note in my pillow case and I hold it all night. *That's* how I can be without you. Not because I don't want you and love you… but because I've incorporated you into my life in ways that you wouldn't even believe."

My tears were hitting the paper so frequently I had to pull it away before I ruined it. He pulled a pillow from behind us and handed it to me.

"Smell it." I put the pillow to my nose and cried even harder. It was sprayed with my perfume. "I spray this pillow with your perfume every few days to feel like you're close to me. I love you, girl. I'm just… loyal as fuck and I couldn't do that to Ced. To be honest with you, Me, that's really why I want to kill your father. Yea, I'm pissed about the possibility of him ordering the hit on my parents, but I've been living my life for this nigga for years and my loyalty to him has cost me you. And for him to do this shit…"

He stood and began to pace. *He really does love me.* I stood and pulled him to me.

"Salem, is this… this is real…"

"Yes, baby. You've always done it for me, Meya. When I tell you I love you I mean that shit."

I turned my back to him and pulled my hair up. His hands massaged my shoulders while he kissed the back of my neck.

"Unzip me, Salem, please," I begged.

I had to have him inside of me – right now! I've always believed that he loved me, but I never thought that he could have possibly loved me as much as I loved him. To know that he did was overwhelming. If I didn't get him inside of me soon I felt like my heart was going to literally liquefy and seep out of my pussy. His lips continued to nip at my neck as his hands squeezed my breasts and I was seconds away from crying.

"Salem," I said louder.

Finally, his hands moved to the zipper of my dress and he slowly pulled it down, but stopped mid-way.

"You fucked that nigga, Meya. How am I supposed to make love to you knowing he's been inside of you?"

"You mean to tell me you haven't had sex with nobody since you took my virginity?"

"No. They suck my dick, but that's it. I haven't had a reason to. Any time I needed some pussy I got it from you." I exhaled, feeling bad as hell. "Was he better than me? You moan that nigga name like you moan mine? That shit is fucking with me, Meya."

"I'm sorry!" I yelled with tears in my eyes. "I'm sorry! But what did you expect, Salem? For the first time in a long time I found someone that can handle me. He knows who my pops is and that hasn't scared him away. He wants to have a future with me. I can't even get you to be my boyfriend while this nigga wants to be my husband. I'm sorry. I never meant to hurt you or make you feel disrespected, but I needed that. I needed to feel loved."

"That nigga don't love you!" He yelled louder than I'd ever heard him yell before. "I love you!"

I took a step back and licked the corner of my mouth.

"I love you too, Salem... but if we can't be together... we have to let each other go."

His eyes lowered. His head tilted back.

"So, what you saying, Me?"

"I'm saying... if you aren't going to commit to me you might as well get used to the idea of me and Nasir because I'm going to be with him."

I hadn't even gotten the shit out of my mouth before my heart started to beat wildly against my chest. Like it knew exactly what I was doing and it didn't want to stay with me if I decided to leave him.

"I appreciate what you've done here tonight and I will never forget this... and I hate to give you an ultimatum... but, Salem, I need more than this. I need more than random nights of sex."

"If you'd rather have what you have with him over what you have with me I can't help but respect that, Meya." He walked over to his dresser and grabbed my keys.

I didn't realize I'd pulled my arms behind my back until he grabbed one and put my keys in my hand. His lips planted the sweetest kiss on my forehead as I wrapped my arms around his neck and allowed my tears to steadily flow.

"I just wanted us to have one night, Meya. One night before our lives changed forever."

"I know and I appreciate you for that, Salem," I managed to spit out as I sobbed.

It didn't matter how much I tried to deny it in my mind, I knew my pops had his parents killed, and he was going to seek the revenge he deserved.

His hands covered my face and he stared deeply into my eyes.

"I love you, girl," he confessed. "If that nigga can give you what I can't..." He closed his eyes and shook his head as if he couldn't believe what he was saying. "I give you my blessing and full support to be with him."

I covered his wrists with my hands and leaned forward to kiss his lips.

"Salem, I promise if I could have you it would be you. You know that, right?"

He nodded and released me. "Go be with your nigga, Me. Go and live your loving happy life and have babies and experience the shit I'll never be able to give you."

Each word that he spoke felt like daggers tossed to my heart. Literally weakening me and making it difficult for me to stand. I stepped to the side and prepared to walk away from the man I swore I'd spend the rest of my life with.

"I'm sorry, Salem..." I mumbled walking away.

"You don't have to apologize, Me. You deserve the good life, baby. You deserve better."

"I only want better if it's better with you. Who better for you than me? Who gone add to your wealth like I do?"

"Shit, who gone water the flowers in your mind like I do?" I smiled softly and turned around to face him. "Go, Me. It's cool, baby. I'm good."

I sighed heavily, nodded, and walked away. Walked away from the man that I never thought I'd be able to tear myself away from.

∞

When I pulled up at my crib and saw Kendrick's car in front of my mailbox I groaned and hit my head against the headrest. Kendrick was cool as hell, but with all that I had going on the last thing I wanted to do was entertain him. Yea, he could've given me some head and took my mind off of things for a few minutes, but I was so drained mentally and emotionally that I didn't even want that shit. I got out of my car and walked over to his. He rolled the window down and I smiled at the sight of him. Pretty ass nigga.

"Hey, what you doing here?" I asked.

"I haven't heard from you in a while. I just wanted to check on you and make sure you were straight. I actually just pulled up a few minutes ago. I was calling you to see where you were, but you didn't answer."

"Yea, my purse and phone are in the trunk."

"Oh, well…"

"It's just been a lot of shit going on, Ken. A lot of shit going on."

"I hear you. You need to get your mind off of it?"

"I do; I swear I do… but not tonight. Can I call you in a couple of days?"

The sadness in his eyes would have made me change my mind, but tonight I didn't even care. If anybody was gone be feasting on me tonight, it was going to be Nasir. At this point, I didn't even want him to because he had cost me my Salem.

"I got you," he mumbled starting his car back up.

I stood back and watched him drive off before going to my trunk and grabbing my phone and purse. I scrolled through my call log and cursed at the missed calls from Nasir. I forgot to send the message telling him I had to switch my flights out. As soon as I got inside of my crib I called him, but he didn't answer. I called a few more times before deciding his ass was just ignoring me.

When I came to that conclusion I booked another flight and prepared to head to Vegas as soon as the sun came up. If I had two more days of peace before my life changed drastically I wanted to spend it with him.

Katara

I was nervous as hell sitting in Ricardo's car. After we had sex he was really forcing this meet the parents shit down my throat. He was standing outside smoking a blunt. He told me I had until he was done to get myself together and then we were going in. Meeting his family just made this seem so… official. Yes, I'd given my virginity. Yes, I can see myself with him for a very long time. Commitment is a scary thing. Commitment automatically leads to expectations and attachment. The way I see it… I can't lose something I'm not attached to. I guess… us not giving this a title and me not meeting his parents was safe to me. If we split I'd be able to say, well… he was never really mine to begin with.

Ricardo came to the door and looked down at me through the window. I smiled and locked it. He had given me his keys to lock it when he got out, but now I was considering leaving his ass here and coming back later.

"Open the door, Katara," he commanded. I shook my head no and sat back in the seat. "You better open this door, girl," he continued as I pulled my phone out of my purse.

He walked into the house and came back after a few seconds. I looked at him and the hammer he had in his hands.

"You would not," I said as he walked to the backseat. "Alright, alright!" I yelled as I unlocked the door. "Crazy ass," I mumbled as I got out of the car.

"You was gonna pay for me to get my window fixed too if I would have had to break it," he said wrapping his arm around my waist.

"Whatever, nigga. No I was not. If your crazy ass wanted to break it that was gon' be on you."

"I can't believe you really don't want to meet my family."

"It's not that I don't want to… I just don't want to *right now*."

"Then when?"

"I don't know. In a year maybe."

"A year? In a year I'll have you barefoot and pregnant." He opened the door and I tried to ignore his last comment. "My folks cool, just relax and be yourself."

"Fine."

He motioned for me to walk in and I shook my head no. I hated when people tried to make me go inside of their home first. Like I knew where I was going. He shook his head again and walked inside. I closed and locked the door behind me and followed him into the kitchen where all the noise was coming from. As if he knew I was considering running out he grabbed my hand.

We walked into the kitchen and the fake smile that I was wearing immediately fell at the sight of my ex – Larry. Larry was the nigga that made me avoid commitment out of fear at all costs. See, Larry lied and played his way into my life in hopes of getting my virginity. He told me everything he thought I wanted and needed to hear to make me fall hopelessly in lust with him. It almost worked too – until I decided to go ahead and cement our relationship.

I went to his place to talk to him about it and give him what he'd so graciously and patiently been waiting for, and I found him in bed with another woman. Now… I ain't gone lie… the shit hurt me bad as hell, but I stayed with him. Larry was the type of nigga that made you question yourself, your worth, and your security when he's the one doing wrong all along.

Larry had me believing it was okay for him to have sex with other women because I wasn't having sex with him. In his twisted way he manipulated me into believing that was okay and for a while I did. He ended up getting some chick pregnant and he broke up with me.

Well, first he ignored my crazy ass. Like he didn't know who my family was. Like I didn't have ways of finding him and her. Then we fought for days on end and he broke up with me. Like I was the one that had fucked up. I said I would avoid that pain from that point forward, and I had been doing a damn good job of doing so.

Larry and Ricardo… they couldn't be brothers. I was hoping he was a family friend that was visiting for some random reason. There was no way they could be related. Sharing the same genes. The same traits. No… they couldn't be brothers.

"Well who is this?" the only lady whom I assumed to be his mother asked.

"This is my girl…"

"Katara James. Long time no see, baby girl," Larry spoke stepping closer to me. I stepped back.

"Larry get the hell away from me," I warned.

"Really, Katara? This how you talk to me after all this time? After all we've been through?"

"How y'all know each other?" Ricardo asked pulling me behind him.

"He cheated on me and got one of them pregnant."

"I didn't cheat. I cheated the first time... but after that it wasn't cheating anymore because you knew about it."

I laughed angrily and took another step back.

"Please tell me you're not related to him," I said grabbing the back of Ricardo's shirt.

"Yea, that's my brother."

I closed my eyes and inhaled deeply.

"I'm ready to go home."

"What? Why? We just got here."

"I don't want to be anywhere near him."

"So it's like that, Katara? You don't love a nigga no mo?" Larry asked with a smile before licking his lips.

"Fuck you!" I yelled before running up on him, but Ricardo grabbed me and carried me out.

"That's alright, Katara! I still love yo young ass! You give my brother what you never gave me? You making him wait like you made me wait? He gone do the same thing I did!"

Ricardo put me down and turned towards his brother.

"Yo, fuck is wrong with you, big bro? You gone respect her because you respect me. Keep all that slick shit from falling out your mouth."

"Alright you two. Just go, Ricardo. Get her out of here. We don't need no drama. No fighting amongst the family. If she's going to cause some drama she will not be invited over anymore," his mother said.

"Trust me, I have no intentions of ever coming back, ma'am. I'm sorry to have momentarily came out of myself, but trust me when I say I won't *ever* be back again."

"If y'all don't want her around y'all don't want me around," Ricardo said wrapping his arm around my shoulders.

As we walked away his mother laughed.

"Oh hush, boy. You know you don't mean that. You'll be back tomorrow. We family. You don't let no outsider come between that."

He ignored her as we continued to walk outside.

∞

The ride to my house was a silent one. I was so pissed and hurt I got out of the car without even giving him a chance to get out and open my door. I was just trying to get away from him.

"Kat... Kat, wait," he called out as he walked towards me.

I opened my door and walked in... leaving it open for him to come inside. I headed straight for the kitchen. I was opening a bottle of Stella Rosa when he made his way inside. He took the bottle from my hands and sat it on the counter.

"I'm sorry," he mumbled pulling me into his arms. "I didn't know."

I couldn't find the strength to hug him back... so I just let him hold me.

"I don't want to come between you and your folks. I don't want to cause any friction. And I'm most certainly never going around your brother again. So... maybe we need to just end this now before this gets too serious."

He released me and tried to look into my eyes but I avoided his.

"Are you fucking serious, Katara? I'm not about to let you use this shit to leave me."

"That's your family..."

"I don't give a fuck! I'm trying to build a family with *you*. I can't marry them. I can't lay up with them. I can't plant no seeds in them. You're my priority. We'll make this shit work. My parents will come around. Larry..."

"I'm not going to be around him. And if you're anything like him... hell... I guess you've gotten the pussy now. So how long is this going to last? You probably knew this whole time. That's why you forced me to meet them because you knew I wouldn't want to have anything to do with him. Now you have the perfect way out."

"Do you know how crazy you sound right now? You think I would go through all of this to get some pussy? They throw it at me on a daily basis, Katara. I'm with you because I want you and everything else you offer. Having your body was a plus. Did you forget all the reasons I said I couldn't get enough of your ass? You think that shit was a game?"

"I don't know. Can you just go? I can't even think right now."

"The hell is there to think about? I didn't know he fucked you over. I'm sorry that he did but I'm not him. I'm not going to do that to you nor will I pay for what he did to you."

"Can you just go?"

He stared at me for a few seconds before taking a step back.

"I get that you're in your feelings right now, so I'm going to go and give you some time to get this shit together in your head... but don't take too long, Katara. I'm not waiting on you for too long."

With that... he walked away.

Meya

When I made it to Vegas I called Nasir and his petty ass ignored me again. I took a cab to his spot and started boiling when I saw his car parked outside. I was knocking on his door and yelling loud as hell. If he didn't want to have anything to do with me that was cool, but he was going to say that shit to my face and give me some closure.

"I know you in there! You better open this door, Salem!" I yelled. "Shit," I mumbled wrapping one hand over the other as if that would take away my last knock and statement. I couldn't believe I called him Salem. I was hoping he didn't hear me, but when he started to unlock the door I knew he had.

He swung the door open and stepped out so fast I tried to step back, but he grabbed me by my shirt and pulled me into him.

"Did you just call me that nigga's name?" Nasir asked in a low and calm voice. So low and calm the shit unnerved me.

"I... it... it just slipped out. Ignoring me is the type of petty shit he does. I wasn't expecting something like this from you."

"The fuck did you expect? The last I talked to you, you were supposed to be on your way here. Your flight gets in and I don't see you. I blow your phone up and I don't hear from you. You were with that nigga... weren't you?"

I exhaled a hard breath and shook my head.

"Nasir, I'm sorry. It's a lot going on. You know that. I just have a lot on my mind. I'm sorry for not communicating with you, but I'm here now."

He looked me over and released me.

"You didn't answer my question."

"Yes, I was with him, but nothing happened. You know after tomorrow shit could get real serious between us. He just... wanted to spend some time with me before that happened, but nothing happened."

"I don't believe you."

"Nasir..."

"But since we aren't in a committed relationship I can't hold that shit against you."

"You're not mad?"

"I'm mad because you didn't communicate with me, Meya. I didn't know what the hell happened to you. I didn't know if you'd missed your flight or if you were here and missing…"

"I'm sorry. I'm sorry."

I was so tired of apologizing I didn't know what to do. I started crying and he pulled me into his arms.

"What's wrong?"

I couldn't tell him the truth. How could I tell him the truth?

"It's just a lot going on, Nasir," I said again.

He pulled me off of his chest only to look into my eyes.

"Let me pull you out of your mind for a couple of days. Let me show you my city and show you the best time of your life. But, you have to open yourself up to me completely and not hold back."

"Please do," I hurriedly agreed.

"Okay, cool. Come on inside and give me a few minutes to get some shit together."

If he wanted to take a shot at making me feel better and getting me to forget about all of the bullshit going on in Memphis, I would happily oblige him.

∞

Nasir and I spent most of the day on the Strip. We gambled, shopped, ate, and gambled some more. It was well after two in the morning when we returned to his place. I checked my phone before hopping in the shower because of course he didn't want me to take it with me when we were out. I had multiple missed calls and texts from Katara. I rushed outside and called her back.

"Hello?" She answered with sleep heavy in her voice.

I let out a sigh of relief when she spoke. I was praying John the Baptist hadn't made a move on her while I was gone. I'd never forgive myself if anything happened to her because of her association with me.

"What the hell happened? You blew my phone up tonight."

"Last night, Me. It's another day now."

I chuckled lightly.

"Okay… well what happened, Kat?"

"You remember Larry?"

My anger rose just at the sound of that bitch ass niggas name.

"Yea I remember him. What about his ass?"

"That's Ricardo's brother."

"What? How you know?"

"I went over to his folks house to meet them and Larry was there."

"Damn. I know your ass acted a fool."

"I tried to swing on um but Ricardo didn't let me."

"What he saying about it? Does he know what happened between y'all?"

"I gave him a brief overview. His mama was like I can't come over if I'm going to be starting drama, so he was like if they don't want me around they don't want him around or some shit. We left and came back to my spot. He was trying to talk about it, but I made him leave."

"Why, Katara?"

"I'm not trying to go through that again."

"You know Ricardo is not like Larry."

"Do I?"

"Larry was a creep ass nigga. His ass was no good. He was a dog. He didn't care about nobody but himself. You know that's not light skinned's style."

I heard the smile on her face as she said, "Do not start calling him that."

"At least it made you smile."

"It did. Lord knows I needed that too. I cried myself to sleep, Me."

"Awww. I'll be back home tomorrow, well later today. You want me to get some niggas to fuck Larry up?"

"Nah. He's not even worth it."

"Aight. Let me know if you change your mind. You know I'll do it. And you need to go back to Ricardo and work this shit out. Obviously you like him. You gave him the pussy. Don't let Larry ruin it. You've wasted enough time and energy on his ass. Let that mane do him and you do you. Fuck if they brothers. Ricardo ain't no standard nigga."

"How you know?"

"I talked to him the first night y'all met. Remember when I said I was going to the bathroom? I went to talk to him and peep him out."

"Knew your ass was up to something. You never use the bathroom when we go out."

"You know I had to check his light skinned ass out before he approached you. Gone go to sleep and get some rest so you won't have any bags under your eyes when you go to make up with your man."

"Speaking of which... where the hell you at? You with Nasir or Salem?"

"Nasir." I walked further away from the door.

"Have you talked to Say?"

"Not today. Not after..."

"Don't go there. Don't give him any of your mental. I hate I even asked. Are you enjoying yourself?"

"Yes, honey. Nasir is that nigga. I can't get enough of his ass. He's so rough and gentle. Street but respectful and reformed. I don't know... if I can't have Salem I definitely wouldn't consider being with Nasir as me settling."

"Good. What did you tell me? You've wasted enough time and energy on Salem. Go forth with Nasir."

"Alright, alright. I didn't call you to talk about me."

"Yea, yea. I love you. I'll see you when you get back."

"Aight, I love you too."

I walked back into Nasir's house and he was cutting a cigar. I wasn't expecting him to smoke since he was a boxer, but I guess there was still a lot about him that I had to find out.

"Come 'ere," he ordered in a low tone.

I went and sat next to him. He pulled my legs on top of his lap and I rested my head on his couch.

"I had so much fun tonight, Nasir."

"Good. The night ain't over yet. You tired?"

"Nah. What you wanna do?"

"Get inside that pussy. You gone let me?"

Nasir looked at me with low eyes and bit his lip. My body reacted without my permission – leaking my juices like it wanted him to drink it up like liquor.

"You know I can't resist you."

"Good. I need you here for my next fight, Meya."

"I will be. Just let me know when. I want to support you. I want to satisfy your needs, but I'm new to this just like you are. I can't fulfill them if I don't know what they are."

He sat his cigar down on the couch and stood, extending his hand for mine.

"So why don't you tell me what you want and need from me and I'll tell you what I want and need from you?"

"That's cool," I agreed as we walked to his bedroom.

We went into his bathroom and he spoke as he undressed me.

"I need you to respect me. To love me. To support me. To encourage me. To be loyal and faithful. To submit. I want you to commit to me. Move in with me. Give me babies. Show me that normal loving part of life that I've never had before."

"Why me?"

"No questions. No fear. No doubt. Tell me what you want and need from me."

My hands found their way to his shirt as I began to undress him.

"I need you to accept me. Love me. Protect me. Never try to change me. Be honest and loyal. Faithful."

"That's it?"

I shrugged and took a step back.

"Yea I guess."

"And what do you want from me?"

"I just want you."

He didn't look like he believed me, and I didn't blame him. Truth of the matter was... I didn't know what I wanted or needed from him. Salem took care of me. Always had... and had it not been for John the Baptist he always probably would.

I didn't know what to ask for or expect from another man because I never really thought about it. Even when I threatened to leave Salem alone completely it never led to this – this... building a foundation with another man. I felt like an alien in a completely different world.

Nasir took a step towards me and took my face into his hands. I looked up at him and licked my lips. Nasir was one fine ass man. My eyes dropped and I ran my hands down his tatted chest, his muscles, and his six pack.

"We can take this as slow as we need to," he assured.

I nodded and covered his wrists with my hands as I looked into his eyes.

"Thank you for being understanding. I want to give you all you want and need... it's just hard for me to depend on you for the same."

"That's understandable. With time you will trust me and trust me to take care of you."

"I'll tell you what I trust you with right now."

"What's that, baby?"

"My body."

"Oh yea? Show me."

Nasir dropped to his knees and pulled one of my legs over his shoulder. He pulled my clit into his mouth and I grabbed the back of his head out of reflex. I thought I could trust this release. I thought this would keep me from thinking about and wanting Salem. But the closer I got to my climax, the more I thought about Salem.

How he looked and sounded when he found out about me giving myself to Nasir. How he told me that he hated me. How Nasir didn't love me... but that he did. The letters. The letters. The pillow that smelled like me. The prom. I cried out as I came and immediately fell into his arms as I sobbed.

Nasir consoled me for a few seconds before picking me up and carrying me to his bed. He climbed in behind me and held me as I gathered myself. The hell was I doing getting head from one nigga then randomly bursting into tears because of the other?

I was tired. Drained emotionally. This shit was breaking me. The business. John the Baptist. My pops. Salem. Nasir.

Nasir.

I turned to face him. He wiped my tears and I smiled softly.

"I'm sorry," I mumbled.

"You wanna talk about it?"

I shook my head no then buried it in his chest. His arm wrapped around me as I threw my leg over his.

"No. I just need you to hold me. I just need something that I know is secure. Everything in my life is shaky right now, Nasir."

"Then I'll be your rock. I will keep you steady."

At the sound of that I lifted my head and looked into his eyes. His fingers caressed my cheek and I closed my eyes in relief.

"I think that's what I need from you most."

"Done."

"And... I need you to want me. To... really want me. And show me that you want me. And have me. And not let anything stand in the way of us. If you want me, Nasir, have me."

Salem and his lack of commitment to me entered my mind, but when Nasir laid me flat on the bed and covered my body with his, those thoughts slowly faded.

"Consider it done, baby. I do want you. And I have absolutely no problem showing you just how much."

For some reason, I believed him. And right now… a man wanting me just as much as I wanted him and not letting anything stand in the way of us was what I needed most.

Katara

The first thing I did this morning was call Ricardo. Literally. Like as soon as my eyes opened I grabbed my phone and called him. I hadn't gotten much sleep between thinking about him and Meya calling me back late as hell. He answered and told me he'd be right over with breakfast. He didn't even sound mad or unconcerned. Really, he sounded just as tired as me.

I had time to shower and put my wet hair in two French braids before he arrived. We sat across from each other at my kitchen table and ate in silence. When we were done he leaned back in his seat and stared at me.

"I'm sorry," I mumbled.

"You don't have to apologize for that, baby. I get that that shit probably brought up some feelings that you weren't trying to have to deal with again."

"Yea, but I shouldn't have taken it out on you. You didn't know. That had nothing to do with you."

Ricardo stood and walked over to me. I stood and he wrapped his arms around my waist.

"Do you trust me?" he asked.

"I do."

"Do you?"

"Yes, Ricardo."

"And you trust that I would never put you in a situation that would hurt you, disrespect you, or make you uncomfortable?"

"I don't think you would do it intentionally."

"I hate that my brother is responsible for the guards you got up, but I'm not paying for no niggas' mistakes. All I'm trying to do is love you. That's it. I have no ulterior motives. I'm not trying to run game. I'm not trying to use you for sex. I'm not cheating on you. I'm not hiding anything from you. I'm not him."

"I don't want to blame you. I don't want this to get in the way of us."

"Us? So there is an us?"

His smile made me smile.

"Yes, Ricardo. There's an us."

"I've been claiming you since the first night we met. Am I your boyfriend yet?"

I connected my fingers behind his neck and rested my arms on his shoulders.

"Yes, baby. You're my boyfriend."

He looked up to the ceiling and thanked God before taking my lips into his and giving me the sweetest kiss he ever had.

"What you got planned today? I want to spend some time with you, Kat."

"Umm…"

My mind traveled to the fact that Meya and Salem were meeting with uncle Ced today. I was more than likely going to have to get up with them when the visit was over. If it was true, all hell was going to break loose. If it wasn't they were going to go into war mode for John the Baptist. Either way I was sure we were going to end up meeting.

"I don't really have anything planned right now, but Meya and Salem will probably be reaching out to me a little later."

"Until then… I want you. I need your undivided attention."

My fingers caressed his cheek softly. The more I had him, the more I wanted him. Not just sexually, but mentally and emotionally. I couldn't get enough of him. I don't know how I thought I would be able to let him go.

"You have me. All of me."

John the Baptist

I watched Salem and Meya stand outside the visiting area and talk. Salem did exactly what I expected him to do. He reacted exactly how I expected him to react. For a nigga like Salem, loyalty was everything. He'd devoted his life to Cedrick, and his pride was not going to allow him to breathe the same air as the man that he felt betrayed him. Played him. Took advantage of him. Underestimated him. Now, they were a few minutes away from watching everything they'd built since Cedrick had been arrested be destroyed.

Meya

I was hit hard in the face with reality as soon as I left the airport and headed to visit my pops with Salem. To go from this peaceful, sensual, and pleasurable exchange with Nasir to this cold, unsure, and nerve wracking feeling was too much to handle. Before we came in, Salem and I talked briefly outside. He told me that he loved me and I told him that I loved him too. I begged him to be rational and loyal no matter what my pops said... but I could tell that shit was going in one ear and out the other.

My pops was the first person to come into the visitation room as usual. Salem's hand covered my thigh and I closed my eyes as tears filled them. The only two men I've ever loved in my life could be seconds away from becoming enemies and there was nothing I could do about it.

"James wants to meet with you in room B," one of the guards on my pops payroll said.

Salem and I stood and followed him to a private room. When we walked in my pops was already seated with his handcuffs off. I looked behind us at the guard who stood in front of the door. Normally I would have tried to get him to give us some privacy... but today I welcomed his presence. I didn't want to have to break up their fight by myself if it came to that.

I sat across from him and Salem remained standing. I had to grab his hand and pull him down to his seat.

"What's up?" pops asked looking from me to Salem.

"You got something you wanna tell me?" Salem asked.

I placed my hand on his forearm and squeezed it gently. He looked at the side of my face and sat back in his seat.

"Spit the shit out, young blood," pops said.

"Pops... Salem was given some information about Ricky Sanders. You were listed as the suspect and his pops was listed as the witness. He thinks you killed his folks to avoid having to go to trial for having Ricky Sanders killed. That's not true... right? It was just a coincidence... right? You didn't have his parents killed... did you?"

Pops scratched the hairs on his chin in silence.

"Own up to the shit. You ain't had a problem before telling us about who you hit. Tell me you did the shit," Salem ordered sitting back up. "Tell me," he continued slamming his fist down on the table.

"Salem, please. Stay cool," I said.

"Fuck that. I wanna hear his ass say it."

My heart started beating fast as fuck. My palms were sweating. My mouth went dry. My legs started shaking. I ain't never been the average chick that gets in her feelings. Hell, it ain't too much that causes me to come out of myself. But this shit... this shit was making me feel things I'd never felt before.

"Your father started working for me when your mother was pregnant with you. He wanted to give you a better life than he had. He hadn't gone to college, and he wasn't making the money that he wanted at his job. Instead of working two and three jobs and not having any time to spend with you and your mom he came to me. Sonny was never a street nigga.

He didn't have it in his blood like you and I do. He wasn't built for this life. I told him that I didn't trust him to hold my weight. He was too nervous. Too jittery. So, I told him that I would find another position for him. Something legal for him to do.

It wouldn't pay as much but I would work with him because he was trying to provide for his family. So, for about sixteen years your father worked for me as my consultant. Sonny was smart as hell. He just... was a lazy motherfucker. I would go to him for counsel on certain things and pay him a couple thousand for each visit. But, then it was time for you to get ready for college.

He wanted more money to be able to send you to school without you getting any loans, and he wanted to get a bigger house for him and your mother after you left. He wanted more money, but like I said... I didn't trust him. He wanted to prove that he could handle this life, so he offered to handle Ricky. Your pops is the one who killed him... not me.

When the police found out they offered your father a deal. Pin the shit on me and he would walk free. Instead of being the suspect he became the witness. Your father was a snitch, Salem."

Pops lit his cigarette and took a few puffs before continuing.

"When I found out that he was working with the police I gave him two options – leave or suffer the consequences of betraying me. I guess he thought because I'd employed him for years that I needed him or some shit. So he stayed. I couldn't let him live. I had to make him a lesson for the rest of my team. He had to go.

You and your mother weren't supposed to be there. He's the reason she's dead. He'd been using her as a human shield practically. Everywhere he went he took her with him. He knew my policy about not killing women and children. She was supposed to be gone to work that Monday morning, but he convinced her to take the day off.

I didn't know until the hit was made and they came back and told me."

"Why didn't you tell him?" I asked in disbelief.

"I didn't know if I could trust him. I didn't know if his heart was like his father's or not. When I brought him into my home I didn't expect him to stay for as long as he had, but there was a hunger and a fire in his eyes that Sonny didn't have.

"Salem, you reminded me of me. I wanted to tell you... but I didn't want you to hold that against me. I said from that point forward that I would be there for you and give you whatever you needed to... to right the wrong of me having your parents killed."

I looked at Salem and searched his face for some type of feeling. He looked at me with those dark, empty eyes and kissed my forehead.

"You know I love you, Me, right?"

I closed my eyes and nodded.

"I know. I love you too."

"Cedrick..." I opened my eyes. That was the first time he'd ever called my pops by his first name when speaking to him. It was Mr. James and then it changed to pops... but never Cedrick. "You think telling me my father was a snitch justifies you killing him and my mother?"

"You know the game. You know what happens to snitches. Fuck it, he wasn't even a snitch his ass was a liar. I could have dealt with him saying I ordered the hit, but he said I pulled the trigger. He put all blame on me and expected me to allow him to continue to breathe while I rotted in prison."

"You're right. You're absolutely right. I know the game. I know you felt like you had to handle it that way, but you know how I have to handle you." Salem stood.

"Do what you gotta do. Let me tell you this, you better use everything I've ever taught you because if you fail and I live… that's it for your ass. Son or not I will kill you."

"I'm not your son. I've never been your son! You're nothing to me!" Salem yelled before walking out.

I stood to run after him but pops stopped me.

"Let him go, baby girl. I need to talk to you."

"No, I need to talk some sense into him."

"Sit down, Meya." I did as I was told and he continued. "John the Baptist?"

"I believe so. The shit was just left on his doorstep one day. It has to be John the Baptist."

"I've never wanted you to run the business, Meya. You know that. I let you learn the business because I wanted you to stay focused on school. I never wanted you to be a part of this shit. Salem is no longer my second in command. He's going to come for me. More than likely he's going to pay a few of these bum ass niggas in here to off me."

"Pops…" Tears were falling rapidly as I stood.

"Listen. I don't want you to take full control. I want you to dismantle the business. Take all that I have stored up and pay my men for their loyalty. Then, I want you to get a legal job as an accountant. Continue on with those apartment complexes. I don't care what you do, just get out the game. Without me and without Salem… there's no one on earth that I trust you and this business with.

Leave the game and live a normal life. Do not try to stop him. Do not try to get even. I deserve this. It's a part of the game. I always knew if he found out he would come after me. I'm going to put up a hell of a fight, and you better believe when my time comes I'm going out like a G."

"No! No! I'm not going to accept this shit! He comes for you he comes for me. Point blank period. If he hires anyone to touch a piece of hair on your head I swear I'm killing him right wherever the fuck he stands!"

"Listen to me, Meya. I am giving you a direct order not to seek revenge. Are you going to disobey your pops?"

"No, pops, but I'm not going to just sit down while he moves on you," I sobbed.

"This is a part of this life, baby girl. I'm surprised I've made it for as long as I have. It was always going to end this way for me. I got too deep. I knew it would be murder or jail for me. You have a chance to get out clean. Salem has a chance to get out clean.

Please, Meya, please. Don't seek revenge. Live your life, baby. Let me be free. Let me get out of this hell hole. Let me be able to be with you in spirit. I'm okay with dying, Meya. This is what I signed up for. Don't worry about me. Promise me that you won't go to war with him."

I shook my head adamantly and stood again.

"I'm sorry, pops, but I can't promise you that."

He sighed heavily and ran his hands over his face.

"Baby, I can't do this if I'm worried about you. At least give me some peace of mind. Promise me that you won't seek revenge."

"Can't you just... be transferred to another facility? Can't you be put in solitary? All I need is some time to calm him down."

"It doesn't matter where I go, baby. He'll be able to find me. Nobody can stop a man with a plan but God."

Defeat washed over my body and pierced my skin with chills. I felt so weak. So helpless. Like I was being drained of my energy.

"So you want me to just accept the fact that the reason my heart bleeds is about to have the reason it beats murdered? Y'all all I got, pops. What I'm gone do?"

"Come on, James. You're well over your designated time," the guard informed us.

Pops stood and walked over to me. He took me into his arms and held me close.

"You will live, baby girl," he whispered into my ear. "You will live."

I went limp and cried even harder – afraid to let go of my father because I knew that would probably be the last time I saw him alive.

Katara

We didn't expect it. We had no way to avoid it. John the Baptist was about to successfully destroy the James empire. He hit us in a place that none of us expected. No place we'd ever be able to protect. No hit we'd ever be able to prepare for. This nigga was good. Too damn good. Meya told me everything that happened when she and Salem went to visit uncle Ced and I was speechless. What was there for me to say? What was there for me to do?

These niggas lived and breathed this street shit. There was no way in hell Salem would just accept the fact that uncle Ced had his parents killed. Uncle Ced understood and accepted that – Meya couldn't. She'd been blowing his phone up and he had yet to answer. I watched her pace back and forth silently. My phone vibrated on the couch so I picked it up and read the text from Salem.

Salem: You with her?

Yes

Salem: Step outside and call me.

I looked at Meya and put my phone in my pocket as I stood.

"I'm about to go and get something to drink and eat. You making me dizzy with all this pacing. What you want?"

"Get me something sweet as hell to drink but heavy. Get me some Port. And some cigars. And some wings from Mike's."

"Aight."

She pulled three hundred dollar bills from her pocket and handed them to me. I waited until I was well down the street to call Salem.

"Kat..." he spoke.

"What's up, Say? Why are you ignoring her phone calls? You know she can't think straight when she doesn't hear from you."

"I can't talk to her, Kat. My mind ain't right right now. She gone protect her pops and I don't blame her for it, but I gotta do what I gotta do."

I gripped my steering wheel harder and groaned.

"Come on, Salem. I know Unc offing your parents was unforgivable, but he's done so much for you. Leave the business, never speak to him again, but don't kill him."

"How am I gon' walk around with that on my back, Katara? Would you be able to live knowing the person that killed your parents was alive? That you'd spent ten years of your life working for them? Loving them? Getting close to their family? Could you handle that shit?"

Lord knows I couldn't... but I wasn't about to tell his crazy ass that.

"But at least he took you in. He groomed you. He loved you. He's done all that a father should for you."

"I don't give a fuck. He's not this great nigga that took a stray in. He a weak ass nigga with a slight conscience. He wouldn't have had to do shit for me if he wouldn't have killed my parents."

"I know, Salem," I replied softly.

"Look, I don't want you in this shit. If Meya wants to come for me she can. I have no choice but to accept that, but I don't want you involved. I shouldn't have to say it... but I'm out the business. I'm not gonna be around to calm her crazy ass down. I'm not gonna be there to protect her. I need you to convince her to get out the game before some shit goes down that she can't handle."

"What? How do you expect me to do that, Salem? This is all she knows. All I know. Yea, I'm trying to go back to school... but I ain't leaving my girl to do this shit alone."

"I'm not asking you to. I'm asking you to get her to stand down. We can handle our shit one on one when the time is right... but I can't stomach the thought of her running the business alone."

I laughed angrily and shook my head.

"You know what, Salem, you don't have to stomach that. You can let this shit go and move on. You could let uncle Ced live and continue on with the business. You're choosing to kill him, but he's not the one that will suffer from it – Meya is. She's not going to stand down, just like she's not going to just let you get away with having him killed. If something happens to her, if she goes to jail... that will be on you for leaving her."

"Just... tell her I love her and I never meant for this shit to end this way. Tell her to stand down, Kat. Please." I pulled over because my vision was blurred by my tears. "Katara..."

"I'm here."

"I love y'all, mane. I promise if there was a way for me to handle this shit and still have her and the business I would, but that's not how it works. If I don't handle this I would feel like less of a man."

"I hear you. I don't agree but I hear you."

"Will you at least try? I can't do it but you can."

"No, you can. Talk to her, Salem. Even if it's just to tell her that you love her and to ask her to stand down. She just wants to talk to you."

"Fine. I will call her or swing through in a day or two. She deserves that much. I just need to think tonight."

"Perfectly understandable."

"Alright, I'll talk to you later."

"Salem…"

"Yea?"

"I love you."

"I love you too, Kat. You take care of yourself. Look after my girl."

"Always."

I ended the call and sat there and just… cried.

Meya

I drunk myself to sleep. When I woke up it was three in the afternoon. My head was throbbing hard as hell. I sat up in the middle of the bed and inhaled the scent of bacon flowing in the air from the kitchen.

"Kat..." I mumbled getting out of bed.

Normally I would have headed straight for the shower, but I needed to tend to this hangover. I walked down the hall to go to the kitchen and get some Pedialyte and was surprised to see Katara stretched out on the couch. I ran back to my room to grab my gun. After resting against the doorframe because of my dizziness I went back to Katara and grabbed her by her shirt.

"Who in the kitchen?" I whispered.

She looked at me briefly and mumbled, "Nasir," before turning over to her side and going back to sleep.

Slowly, I walked back to my room, put my gun back, and went into the bathroom. After showering I went back to check on Kat. Her ass was knocked out. I don't know who went to sleep and when... but we both had a long night.

Nasir was sitting at my kitchen table eating fruit like this was his house. I stopped by the stove and grabbed a piece of bacon off of the plate he had in the middle of it and sat next to him.

"What you doing here?" I asked after taking a bite.

"You don't remember calling me last night?"

"What? Nah. When?"

"Around twelve. I came over and your cousin let me in. I put you to sleep, held you, and got up this morning to go workout. When I came back y'all were still sleep so I figured smelling some breakfast would wake you up."

I smiled softly and covered my face. I gotta stop drinking so damn much. All this drunk dialing was not cool.

"Thanks for coming and for cooking. Yesterday was crazy as hell."

"You wanna talk about it?"

"Nah. Not really. If I could forget it I would."

I kissed his cheek and hugged him.

"Whatever it is I'm sure it will work out," he mumbled into my ear.

"I hope so. What you cook?"

I released him and stood.

"Bacon, hash browns, grits, and I chopped some fruit."

"Damn. I need you over more often. Thank you. Has Kat been up at all?"

"Nah."

"Let me get her up so she can eat. Thank you, Nasir. You don't know how much you being here means to me. I guess I needed you last night. I don't remember calling you... but I'm glad you came."

"It's cool. I'm sure you would have done the same for me."

I smiled and inhaled deeply.

"Absolutely."

When I returned to the couch I shook Katara gently until she stirred.

"Go away, Me," she whined turning her back to me.

"Get up, Kat. You need to eat. And we need to talk."

She opened her eyes weakly.

"About what?"

"If Salem is out... I..." I turned and looked towards the kitchen. "I might need you to take on a bigger role, but only if that's something that you're comfortable with."

"I'm down. Just... get out my face right now so I can sleep. We can talk later."

I smiled and pinched her cheek until she smacked my hand away.

"Gone, Me!"

"Fine! Grouchy ass lil girl. I bet you don't talk to that light skinned nigga like this when he wakes you up."

She opened her eyes again and I smiled harder.

"Stop calling him that. And that light skinned nigga wakes me up with the dick. All you have to offer is what?"

"Food. You don't smell that shit?"

Her eyebrows wrinkled and she inhaled deeply as her eyes closed again.

"I didn't even pay that shit no attention. Okay, I'm getting up."

Katara

I didn't plan on leaving Meya alone, but I felt like I could trust Nasir with her. By the time I made it home it was close to five and Ricardo had been blowing my phone up. I shot him a text and told him to come over and that I would explain everything as much as I could when he got there.

When he arrived he had the biggest attitude ever. It was kind of cute. I didn't want to make him even madder by smiling and laughing so I held it in as he walked past me and into my bedroom. I slowly walked behind him and planned on explaining the shit before he went off and said something we both would regret.

"Why the hell you ain't been answering the phone, Kat? And I rode by here three times yesterday and your ass wasn't here. You fucking off on me?"

I sat on the edge of my bed and motioned for him to sit next to me. He sat on my bean bag across from the bed. I crossed my ankles and my arms over my chest. We could play this game all night if he wanted to, but I wasn't saying shit until he sat next me. His ass realized that and came and sat next to me.

"No I'm not fucking off on you, Ricardo. It was some family shit going on. I guess you could say it was kind of a crisis. I was with Meya. I'm sorry for not communicating with you, but it was crazy and it just slipped my mind to connect with you." I grabbed his hand and kissed his lips softly and quickly. "You forgive me?"

"I guess. Don't do that shit no more, though. I didn't know what happened to you."

"I'm sorry. I didn't mean to have you worrying. It was just crazy, baby."

"Is it taken care of now?"

"Not at all. It's nowhere near being taken care of."

"Well… I know she in the streets, but I don't need you in that shit with her. If something happened to you because of her that would fuck me up. I know we just met but I've gotten close to you, girl. I don't want to lose you."

I smiled and caressed his cheek.

"Nothing is going to happen to me."

"You don't know that. Bullets have no name on them, and the feds don't care who they get. They just want somebody from the team."

"It won't be me, but that's my blood. I'm riding with her til the wheels fall off, and even then I'm helping her push this shit until she's ready to stop."

"Ain't this some shit. Usually it's the woman begging the man to leave the streets... not the other way around."

I smiled harder as I straddled him.

"I don't even want to talk about that right now. I'm not in the business. I'm just her assistant. You have nothing to worry about."

"Promise?"

"I promise."

"Good."

His lips covered mine and I allowed him to ease my mind for this moment in time.

Meya

To say that I was surprised to see Salem's face on my screen this morning would be the ultimate understatement. Honestly, I was so surprised I couldn't even answer the phone. I just... watched until the call ended. That snapped me out of my trance and I quickly called him back.

Basically he said that he wanted to see me. To spend some time with me. The sadness in his voice let me know that he'd come up with whatever he planned on doing to gain his revenge. As hard as it was for me to accept that fact, I agreed to see him.

If all I had was one day... one night... I would willingly accept it. My father wasn't a factor. Nasir wasn't a factor. The business wasn't a factor. All I wanted was one night with my love. My best friend. My heart. My everything. Before he did the unthinkable and crushed my soul.

He picked me up around eight in the morning and told me to dress casually, so I put on sweats, Nike flip flops, and one of his tee shirts that were at my house. My hair was in a messy bun at the top of my head. Not because I wanted it to be, but because I was tossing and turning so much in my sleep that it looked a hot damn mess when I woke up this morning.

When he made it to my house... he rang the doorbell. He rang the doorbell. And he didn't just let himself in. Salem waited there. Outside. For me to let him in. I stood in my bedroom and waited for him to walk in, but he never did.

My eyes were about to flood over with tears, but I refused to let them fall. I grabbed my purse and headed to the front door.

The sight of him literally took my breath away. Like... I literally couldn't breathe. He took a step towards me and my heart pounded against my chest. His hand cupped my cheek and the tips of his fingers caressed it.

I shivered under his touch at the same time his lips covered mine. The kiss was so soft and quick I almost missed it, but the tingling in my lips as I opened my eyes confirmed that it was there. That he was there.

"You ready?" Salem asked.

I nodded and grabbed my doorknob to close it behind us.

He drove to Sikeston, Missouri. To Lamberts. My favorite freaking place to eat in life! We ate so much we had to sit there for about thirty minutes before getting up to leave. After that we made our way back to Memphis, well, Southaven, and we shopped.

I shopped. He paid.

Then he took me to a spa where he selected the Royal Treatment package for me. It took seven hours for me to receive the whirlpool bath, full body massage, facial, lunch, Seaweed body treatment, and deluxe manicure and pedicure treatment that was included in the package. By the time I left I was so relaxed I just wanted to go home and pass out, but that wasn't all he had in store for me.

He pulled up to my crib and pulled a few boxes and bags from his trunk.

"Salem... this is too much," I acknowledged with tears filling my eyes.

Salem didn't say anything. Honestly, he hadn't said much while we were at Lamberts or at the mall. He just, grabbed the stuff, went to my front door, and waited for me. I let him in and he put the bags and boxes on my bed.

"Dinner will be at my place. So take as long as you need to get ready. Just call me about fifteen minutes in advance from when you're ready and I'll come back to get you."

"Salem?"

"Yea, Me?"

"How are we going to do this?"

He shrugged and looked away from me.

"You'll find a way."

Salem turned to leave, but stopped and walked back towards me. I looked up at him in time enough to watch his lips lower to my cheek. I twisted my face so that his kiss landed on the edge of my lips. He kissed there again. And again. His forehead rested on mine as we both inhaled a deep breath.

"Can't you just not..."

His finger shut my lips and silenced me. I took a step back and he unwillingly walked away slowly.

I think I drank half a bottle of wine as I soaked in my tub. Trying to drown my thoughts, but it didn't work. I was so fucked up over Salem I was really weighing my options. Could I learn to accept the fact that he killed my pops? With him out of the way there would be nothing stopping Salem and I from being together.

The fuck am I kidding? There's no way in hell I could lay next to the man that ordered the hit on my father. No matter what my pops did.

And then there was Nasir. The man that came from out of nowhere. The man that was willing to give me everything I wanted and needed... but no lie... if the shit wasn't coming from Salem it felt artificial.

You don't love the one you love; you love the one that loves you.

Nasir's words were ringing in my ears so loud I quickly washed myself and got out of the tub. I cut some Jhene Aiko up loud enough to try and block the thoughts out as I got ready. When I was done putting my body butter on I began to open the bags and boxes one by one. I put the smallest one to the side for last.

The first bag held a Josh Goot single jacquard weave waist tuck pencil dress. He knew I loved anything Jacquard. It was a sleeveless black and white dress that hugged my body perfectly when I tried it on. The basket weave design, low cut back, and form fitting material made me feel so sexy. So classy. So much like a woman. In the box was a pair of black Christian Louboutin heels. In the smaller bag was a black Alexander McQueen floral knuckle satin clutch.

The medium box had a black choker necklace and a pair of gold diamond studs.

Something told me to open the smallest box when I was done getting ready, so I flat ironed half of my hair, then texted him and told him to come. He arrived twenty minutes later and I was putting the finishing touches on my makeup.

I sat on the edge of my bed and opened the smallest box. It was his key to my house. Tears threatened to spill yet again, and had I not just done my makeup I probably would have let them. But I stood and made my way to the bathroom to grab some tissue. A few sprays of Chanel no. 22 later I was opening the front door and locking it behind me.

He smelled good. And I'm sure he looked good. But I couldn't pull myself to look at him. All looking at him would do was make me want to cry. We walked to his car silently and he opened the door for me. The ride to his home was a silent one.

The fact that I knew that this would probably be my last peaceful visit had my damn eyes watering again. This time, I let them fall as I waited for him to open the door for me, but I quickly wiped them away before I got out.

I got out of the car, still avoiding his eyes, but he wrapped his arm around my stomach and kept me from walking towards the door. I looked up at him and our eyes met. He looked at me briefly before removing his arm and closing the door behind me. Each step I took towards his house felt like bricks hitting my heart.

Strings unraveling from my soul. This was what I wanted – to have this soul tie removed. To be free of him if we couldn't be together. But the closer we got, the weaker I felt. The more open my heart and soul felt. But it wasn't a good open. It was a full and consuming open. An open that made me feel like I would burst inside. An open that filled me inside. An open that left room for me to feel nothing else but the love and desire I had for Salem Myers.

He unlocked the door and I stepped inside. My mind immediately traveled back to the last time I was here. Prom.

Salem led me to his dining room where he served me. I ate slow. Afraid that this was the end. That after this he would tell me what he had planned for my pops then take me home. The thought made me lose my appetite. I pushed the plate away from me and leaned back in my seat.

Salem took a sip of his Hennessey and leaned back in his seat.

"Something wrong with the food?" he inquired.

I shook my head no as my leg shook.

"It's good."

"Then why aren't you eating?"

"I don't have much of an appetite, Salem."

He placed his elbows on the table and ran his hands down his face before linking his fingers together and putting them under his chin.

"When I dropped you off at the spa... I was tempted to be like fuck this shit. Just snatch your ass up and just... leave Memphis. Never looking back."

"Why didn't you?"

"I'm a man, Meya. I'm a street nigga. The man that I've devoted the past ten years of my life to betrayed me in a way I never thought was possible. I can't just let that shit slide, baby."

"Not even for me?"

"When I kill him... will your love for me keep you from coming after me?"

I lowered my eyes and shook my head.

"There you go, Me."

Salem stood and walked over to me. He held his hand out, and I placed mine inside. I stood and he wrapped his arms around my waist.

"You know I love you, Me, right?"

"I know. I love you too, Salem. Too fucking much."

"Can you be mine... just for tonight?"

"I will always be yours. No matter what."

With that, Salem grabbed my hand and led me to his bedroom. I wasn't expecting this day to end with sex. Not since I was still messing off with Nasir. Salem made it perfectly clear the last time I was here that he didn't appreciate the fact that I'd given myself to another man.

He sat on his bed and pulled me in front of him. My hands ran down the back of his head as he looked up at me. I couldn't help but smile. The love that was only there with my pops and I was shining brightly. Salem smiled, as if he knew it too, and kissed my forearm.

"Strip for me," he mumbled.

I took a step back and watched him watch me. His hazelnut skin. His wavy fade. His eyes. Those dark eyes. His full skin colored lips. His scar. Wait what? I made my way back over to the bed and kneeled before him. There was a small barely noticeable scar on the top left of his lip. Normally his mustache goatee combo was longer and thicker, but it was low and freshly cut today. I ran my pointing finger over it and he closed his eyes.

"What is this from?" I wondered.

His hand grabbed mine as he looked down into my eyes.

"Kevin."

My mind traveled back immediately. When I was twenty, I met Kevin. He was a cool nigga. Always smiling. I thought he was a cool, normal dude, so I let him take me out on a date. But that nice guy act quickly faded when I told him that I wasn't interested in having sex with him. He tried to take what he wanted, and I proceeded to beat his ass.

When I got home I got sloppy drunk. I don't remember what happened that night, but when I woke up, Salem was holding me. He asked me what the hell happened and I told him. He told pops and pops gave Salem permission to handle Kevin. But that didn't explain why he had that scar.

"What about him?"

"That night... when I found you... I nudged your shoulder to wake you up and you spazzed out on me. You smacked the shit out of me with the back of your hand. Cut the top of my lip with your ring. You were screaming and crying and... I just refused to believe a nigga had violated you, but that's the way you were acting. Like you didn't even know who I was. Like you didn't recognize my touch.

Eventually I got you to settle down and you went back to sleep. I got up and took care of the cut, then slept with you until the next morning."

"How could I have not noticed that?"

"You were in your own world for a few days after that, Me. You didn't notice hardly anything. You probably just didn't pay it any attention. By the time I was done handling that nigga and shit it had a scar on it anyway."

"That was years ago. I must have hit you pretty hard for the scar to still be there. I'm so sorry."

Salem smiled and grabbed my arms to lift me to my feet.

"Strip for me," he repeated.

I removed my dress, my bra, my panties, my shoes. Until I was down to nothing. And for the first time... I was insecure under his stare. He stood and towered over me. But I couldn't look into his eyes. I wouldn't look into his eyes.

"I'm going to miss everything about you, Me. But this body..." His hand traveled down my waist to my hip and right thigh. "Inside of your body is where I find the most peace."

My eyes closed as chills pierced my skin.

"Look at me," he pleaded.

I shook my head no and tried to take a step back, but he wrapped his arm around my waist and pulled me close.

"Look at me, Meya."

I looked into his eyes and he cupped my cheeks into his hands.

"I want you to leave the business," he said softly.

My body tensed. I tried to remove myself from him, but he held my face tighter.

"The fuck would make you say that shit?"

"Just as naked and vulnerable as you are now is just how naked and vulnerable you will be in the streets without me and Cedrick."

"Salem... I'm not leaving. The business is secure."

"Secure? The hell do you think is going to happen to you when me and Cedrick are out of the way? You will be a clear target for John the Baptist. Your ass will be walking right into a trap if you continue to do business."

"I appreciate your concern, but I'm not standing down. If you care that much don't leave me. Don't take him from me. From us. I know what he did was fucked up, but he loves and cares about you."

"I don't want to hear that shit, Me. I just want you to leave the streets. I won't be able to function worrying about when John is going to make his move on you. Him getting to you will destroy me."

"Let me get this straight... it's not okay for him to come after me, but it's okay for you and I to go to war?"

"Neither is okay. I'm not asking for war with you. If you want to take it there after I do what I have to do I have no choice but to retaliate. That doesn't mean that's something I want, though."

I massaged my temples as my head began to pound.

"I really don't want to talk about this, Salem. Can you just... make love to me?"

Instead of putting up the fight I knew he would, Salem removed his clothing and carried me to his bed. He opened the drawer of his bedside table and pulled out a condom and I chuckled in anger. We'd never used a condom before. Ever. That shit shouldn't have fazed me so much... but it did.

"So we wearing condoms now, Salem?"

"You fucked another nigga."

"He ain't give me nothing!"

"How am I supposed to know that?"

"Because I'm telling you! I wouldn't be reckless like that. Putting your health in jeopardy would be putting my health in jeopardy."

He nodded, but kept the condom in his hand.

"You know what... fuck this shit. Can you just take me home?"

"Why?"

"Because this is stupid."

And it's breaking my heart.

"I wanna wear a condom and it's stupid?"

"No! It's stupid because you rang my damn doorbell!" I yelled with tears running down my face. "You rang my doorbell, Salem. Then you give me the key to my house back. Now you want to wear a condom?"

"Ain't that what you wanted? How many times have you told me not to just walk in? How many times have you asked for your key back, Me? Do you know how many times you've gotten the locks changed?"

"So! I didn't mean that shit!"

His shoulders relaxed as he put the condom on the table.

"I don't know what the fuck you want from me, Me."

"I just want you. That's it."

"What about that nigga? What about..."

"Fuck Nasir. Fuck my pops. In this moment all that matters to me right now is you."

It was as if his brain disconnected from his heart, and he finally allowed himself to feel. His body was on top of mine before I could prepare. His tongue found its way inside of my mouth and connected with mine. A moan escaped my throat at the contact, and that just made him kiss me harder. Deeper.

Salem pulled his mouth from mine and looked at me. Really looked at me. Like there was something about me that he was trying to brand into his brain. His mouth opened to speak, but he placed soft yet hard kisses all down my neck. My chest. My stomach. Licking and biting every part of me that wasn't kissed.

His hands wrapped around my thighs as he bit them. Licked them. Sucked them so hard I was sure I'd have hickeys by the time he was done with me.

Salem looked up at me with a mischievous grin. He was marking me. Daring another man to make his way between my thighs. Where only he truly belonged. My eyes closed and I bit down on my lip the second his mouth closed around my clit. Shit. Lord knows I was gonna miss this. It wasn't just about sex. It was... the way... he pulled me out of myself. In a good way.

In his arms. In his mouth. Around his dick. I was always able to unravel. And be myself. Be a woman. Be emotional. Be satisfied. Be full. Be normal. Be loved.

That familiar quake had begun to slowly rumble within me when Salem stopped and prepared to enter me, but I stopped him and laid him on his back. I trailed my fingers up and down his thighs and watched as he moved his head from side to side. Trying to contain the desire that was building within him.

My tongue swirled around the crown of his dick and my emotions almost got the best of me. All my life I'd been raised to view myself as a Queen. As royalty. To go after what I wanted and to not allow anyone to rob me of it or my peace and happiness. To not seek acceptance from anyone or be swayed by their rejection.

I was groomed to be the Queen of the streets. Right alongside my King. And the one that handed his kingdom down to us was also the reason one of us was about to be dethroned.

"Get out your mind, Meya. Stay in this moment with me."

I looked up at him and realized I was gripping his dick and doing nothing else with it. With a deep breath I closed my eyes, fighting back my tears, and took his entire length in my mouth.

"Shh…"

The curse that was supposed to come out of his mouth was replaced with a sharp intake of breath as I locked my cheeks around him and sucked as hard as I could while pulling him out of me. He only allowed me to do that once more before he was pushing me away from him and laying me flat on my back.

Then he entered me with one slow, deep stroke. His arms wrapped around me and he lifted me a couple of inches off of the bed as he stroked me so soft and long and deep I thought my body was about to fucking fall apart.

I wrapped my arms around his neck. My legs around his waist. Buried my head into his neck. And held on with all that was in me.

The sound of his body ramming into mine. The sound of my nectar spilling out of me and on to him. His grunts and moans in my ear. His fingers digging into my sides. His arms holding me tighter. Closer. The speeding up of his strokes. It was… it was all too much. Too much. Too fucking much.

My legs began to shake and I came hard. And long. He placed me back on the bed and ran his fingers down my chest and stomach as I struggled to catch my breath. When I had it he smiled and put one leg on his shoulder while gripping the other that remained around his waist.

"Ima miss you, Meya," he admitted in the softest voice I'd ever heard him use.

I turned my head to the side and closed my eyes as he began to stroke me again. So slow. So soft. So long. Then so fast. So hard. So deep. My back arched and he went even deeper as he moaned.

He pulled out and licked his lips as he looked down at me.

"I said Ima miss you," he repeated.

I smiled and pulled him down to me.

"Ima miss you too, baby."

He licked and nibbled on my lips before sliding his tongue back into my mouth. I stroked his back and wrapped both legs around him as I lost myself in our kiss. His kiss. No one kissed me like Salem Myers. No one handled me like Salem Myers. No one loved me and protected me like Salem Myers.

I flipped him over so that he was on his back and I lowered myself on top of him. We both moaned as he gripped my hips and kept me in place.

"Don't go fast or I'll nut," he said.

Going fast was the last thing I planned on doing. I wanted to make this last. I needed to make this last. I lifted and lowered myself on him as slow and deep as I possibly could. For the first few strokes I was able to look into his eyes, but it started getting too good. I started getting too hot. And my eyes closed as my head flung back.

Even when he grabbed my hair and pulled me down to him they remained closed.

"Don't you cum, Me."

"I'm trying not to, but you feel so good, Say."

He pulled my hair harder as his arm wrapped completely around my waist and I moaned.

"Shit, Salem," I moaned speeding up.

"Don't."

My whimper was my response. He lifted his body and matched my strokes, which only made me grip him tighter.

"Meya," he moaned into my ear. "Fuck, baby."

The sound of his hand slapping my ass sounded off against the walls of the room.

"I love you, Salem," I moaned as I felt myself surrendering to my orgasm.

"I love you too, Meya."

Salem flipped me over and stroked me until I came. And he came right along with me. We laid there for a few seconds. With him on top of me. Feeling our breathing and heart beats sync. I tried to pull myself from under him to shower, but he pushed me back down.

"I need to take a shower."

"Later. Just... lay here for a minute."

I nodded and ran my hands up and down his back. He placed a kiss on my shoulder before wrapping both arms around me. My legs wrapped around his waist. And in the most awkward position we'd ever been in... both physically and emotionally... I drifted off into the most peaceful sleep I'd ever had before.

Katara

Meya told me that she wanted us to meet up and talk this morning, so I was at her place before my first meeting with Marlon and Derrick. When I called her and she didn't answer I used my key to get in. Her car was in the garage, but she was gone.

We were supposed to have breakfast at eight, but her ass didn't roll up until nine. In the passenger's seat of Salem's car! I was about to leave her and head out for the meeting, but seeing them together made me glad I stayed. I started to get out of my car and dance, but they both were so stubborn that I didn't want to get too happy too soon. What I was hoping and praying was a reconciliation that meant no one was going after anyone could have easily been a one last night together type of thing.

Salem got out of the car and winked at me as he walked over to Meya's side. She got out and they shared a quick kiss before he wrapped his arms around her waist. His chin rested on the top of her head and I looked away. I was about to get in my feelings and it was too early in the morning for that. They both walked over to my car hand in hand. I rolled the window down and Me spoke first.

"Just give me two minutes to go in the house and throw on some shorts or something."

"Not no little ass shorts either," Salem ordered as Meya walked away.

Normally she'd have something smart to say, or she'd mug him, this time she just looked back at him sadly and nodded.

"The hell was that about?" I questioned.

He leaned down and put the palms of his hands on the car.

"Shit. She probably just... I don't know."

"Y'all cool now?"

Salem shook his head no and looked towards the door.

"I gotta do what I gotta do, Kat."

"So you're really going to do this? You're really going to have uncle Ced taken care of?" He didn't answer me, but the look in his eyes told me that he was. "Then what?"

"That's up to her. I asked her to leave the business, but she declined. If she wants to come after me that's completely understandable, but I'm praying that she'll just... let this shit go. All of it."

"You expect her to let this shit go and you can't?"

"If you need anything, Kat, you know how to get in touch with me. Nothing has changed between us."

I looked away from him and shook my head as tears filled my eyes. This was not supposed to be happening. Meya came back out in some knee length jersey knit shorts and Salem smiled.

"The first time she wanna listen to a nigga and it's more than likely gone be the last."

He shook his head and lifted himself from my car. Salem walked over to her and opened the door for her.

"You know I love you, Me, right?"

"I know, Salem. I love you too. If you change your mind..."

"I won't."

"Then I guess this is it, huh?"

"I guess so."

He pulled her into his chest and whispered something into her ear that I couldn't hear. She gripped his arm and squeezed tightly as her knees buckled. Salem's grip around her waist tightened and he kept her from falling. Her shoulders started to tremble from crying and the tears that I was holding finally began to fall.

She held him closer. Tighter. Harder. She cried louder. And I couldn't take that shit.

"Me, we gotta go, baby," I said as I opened my door to walk over to her.

Salem looked at me and for the first time... since I'd met him ten years ago... I saw him cry. I couldn't believe he was shedding some tears too.

He removed Meya's arms from around him and handed her to me.

"I love you, Meya. I swear I do. I'm so sorry, baby. But this is something I have to do."

She didn't answer him. She just fell into my arms and cried on my shoulder. Salem took a step back, but stood there for a second before wiping his face and going to his car. I don't know how long we stood out there crying, but when she gathered her strength she pulled herself up and got into my car.

We wiped our faces and sat there for a good long while before I started the car and headed to Waffle House. At that moment, the business and my meeting with Marlon and Derrick didn't matter. My only concern was my cousin's emotional wellbeing.

"Listen…" She spoke. "Shit is about to get ugly, Kat. If Salem has my pops murdered I have to retaliate."

My eyes closed immediately.

"I don't want to… Lord knows I don't… but as of now… Salem Myers is the enemy. I don't have him anymore. I don't have my pops here to help me with the business. So I need you to be more than my assistant. I need you to be more like my right hand woman."

"Doing what exactly?"

"I need you to take my place as the accountant while I take Salem's place heading everything else."

"Meya…"

"You won't be in any more danger as the accountant than you're in as my assistant."

"I don't give a fuck about that!" I yelled louder than I wanted to. I closed my eyes and inhaled a deep breath. "You're sitting here telling me the man you love is about to have your father murdered, and how you're going to have to go after him because of it, and the only thing you're concerned about is the business?"

"What else am I supposed to do, Kat? I can't dwell on that shit. There's nothing that I can say or do to change Salem's mind. My focus right now needs to be on the aftermath of what's about to go down. People will expect me to fold without Salem…"

"If you're even alive! What if he kills you?"

"He won't."

"How do you know? You think he's going to just let you kill him?"

"Katara, I'm not trying to think about that right now, okay? Maybe he'll leave as soon as he orders the hit. Maybe he'll go somewhere where I won't be able to reach him. He can live his life and I can live mine."

"When has Salem ever ran or backed down from a problem?"

"Never," she mumbled softly.

I grabbed her hand and lowered my voice.

"You know I'm riding with you. Whatever you need me to do I will do. But what I'm not going to do is sit around while you two kill each other. Physically, mentally, or emotionally. I'm not saying uncle Ced deserves to die, but I am saying Salem deserves his revenge. Can you imagine how this has been eating at him? Meya... uncle Ced gave you a direct order not to retaliate. This is a part of the game, baby. Let this shit go. Leave the game. Leave Salem the hell alone. And let's get this money the legal way."

"I can't. I'm sorry. I may consider leaving the streets at some point, but there's no way in hell I'll ever be able to just sit on the fact that Salem or anyone else ordered a hit on my pops. I can't. I don't care what he told me to do. If Salem makes his move... I have to make mine."

My reply was cut off when our waitress came to take our drink orders. My stomach caved in. Not from hunger. But from fear. Either way it went, I was about to lose at least two of the closest people to me.

John the Baptist

It felt good as hell to complete a successful job. Even though the shit with Cedrick, Meya, and Salem wasn't over yet there was no doubt in my mind that it would be over soon. Salem was going to kill Cedrick. Meya was either going to go after him and they would end up going to war, or she would dismantle the organization and leave the game behind. Either way... the way would soon be clear for my client to take over Memphis and Cedrick's business.

Normally I didn't overthink the completion. I made moves to start on my next job, but because Meya and Salem were so close I wanted to make sure I was straight on all sides. So, before I got my day started with my lady, I called Omen and told him that the job was done. That no one knew who I was still. But if for some reason anything happened to Nasir... it would be because of my life as John the Baptist. If anything happened to John the Baptist it would be at the hands of Cedrick, Salem, and Meya.

I didn't want Meya to be in her head overthinking this shit. I didn't want her to have time to think of a way to save her father or the business, so I was keeping an even closer eye on her than usual. After Katara left I had Meya to get dressed so we could go out. We went to a couple of stores and grabbed something to eat before heading to Alchemy for drinks.

Let me be honest, when I approached Meya a little while back at L.O.V.E... I didn't plan on it. It was never my plan to get close to her. It was never my plan to reveal my true identity to her. No one knew that John the Baptist was Nasir Patterson. I always planned on keeping it that way, but there was just something about Meya that had me doing things I didn't normally do. I never wanted a normal life – until I met her. I never told a woman about my past – until I met her.

Everything that I told her and did with her was true and sincere. I did want to spend my life with her. I did want her to have my babies. I just... never wanted her to find out that I was the reason she had to leave the streets. That was business, but what we had going on was personal. And I never wanted the two to intertwine. As long as I could finish this last job without her finding out that I was John the Baptist I'd be home free. She would leave the game and be the woman by my side, and I'd be able to continue to live my double life.

Cedrick

I knew my daughter well enough to know that no matter how much I told her not to try and stop Salem or go after him when all was said and done that she would do both. So, I made it my mission to find out as much about this John the Baptist nigga that I could. Looking for information on him led to a dead end, so I directed my attention to what he used to cause the rift.

Salem. Salem's father. The hit that started it all. Ricky Sanders.

Nothing crazy was sticking out to me about that hit. It was supposed to be a regular hit. A regular personal hit. A hit I wanted to do myself, but let Salem's father do to prove his worth. The only reason it went south was because Salem's father turned out to be a liar and a fucking snitch.

Then I went back as far as I could and thought about who would want to dismantle my organization. Who in Memphis had the money to hire John the Baptist? And then… it hit me. As risky as it was, I called Salem and told him that he needed to visit me ASAP.

He came the next day and sat in front of me with a look of disgust covering his face. Salem would never understand why I did what I did, and in a sense… I completely understood that and his anger. I guess… me looking out for him was my way of making what I did right. I at least thought he would be able to have his mother, but she was just at the wrong place at the wrong time.

I never thought I could replace his father, but over the years I did all that I could to fill that void. And for a while… it seemed like it was enough. Like I was enough.

"What you need?" he asked me.

"I know who hired John the Baptist… and why."

Meya

Nasir was making this situation easy for me just by spending time with me and getting me out of my head. I don't know how I'd be handling this shit without him and Kat. He and I were having drinks at Alchemy before we headed back to his place. I was more than ready and willing to get in his bed and lay up with him.

Salem hadn't made any moves yet. My pops was still breathing. So I was going to enjoy this peace that he was offering me for as long as I could. Shit was going to get real, real soon, and I was in no rush to deal with it.

Salem was quiet and lethal when he struck. He struck quick and when you least expected it. My pops trained him well. And it's crazy how his protégé was about to turn the tables on him.

"You ready, baby?" Nasir asked.

"Yea, I'm ready."

Nasir stood and I did as well. His arm wrapped around my waist and he led me out of the restaurant. I saw a nigga that looked vaguely familiar standing at the door. I was hoping he wasn't who I thought he was. Pete had a bad ass habit of talking mad shit. I used to be crazy about his ass. Well, I was crazy with his image and his music.

A while back I went to one of his concerts with Kat and got to go back stage to kick it with him. His energy and character was not like I expected. I let him eat the pussy but that was it. He threw me a few stacks to impress me, but that shit didn't work. I had my own money so his didn't impress me. I gave him Kat's number and he had her phone going off the meter he was calling so much. It got to the point that she had to get it changed.

Whenever I saw him out he always tried to start some shit out of pride. I was hoping he didn't try that tonight while I was with Nasir. I had enough drama going on. I didn't need him adding on to it. We made it to the door and sure enough it was Pete. I rolled my eyes and grabbed Nasir's hand.

"What's wrong?" he asked looking down at me.

"Nothing," I mumbled putting my head down so Pete wouldn't notice me.

"Oh... so that's what the fuck we doing? I pay you to get rid of her ass and you end up fucking her? Type of shit is that, John?" Pete asked.

I looked at him to see who he was talking to and he was looking at Nasir. His ass had to be confused.

"What the fuck are you talking about, Pete? And who you talking to?"

I released Nasir's hand and stepped towards Pete.

"This nigga."

Nasir pulled me behind him and pushed Pete out of the way. He tried to walk out of the restaurant, but I let go of his hand.

"Nah, I wanna hear what he got to say," I said turning around to face Pete. "What you talking about? Did you call him John?"

"He got me confused with somebody else. Don't you?" Nasir questioned with a quiet but stern voice.

Pete looked from me to Nasir.

"Yea. I uh... my fault."

He tried to walk away but I stopped him.

"Why did you call him John?" I asked as Nasir grabbed my hand.

"I just said he had me confused with somebody else. Let's go."

"Fuck that!" I yelled as I jerked my hand away from him. The wheels in my head started spinning. It was all starting to make sense. "Pete, say what the fuck you got to say or I'm putting a bullet in your head tonight," I warned putting my hand on my purse.

"Fine. I called him John because that's who he is. John the Baptist. I hired him to destroy you. What I didn't plan on was him taking your ass out on dates and shit on my dime."

I heard him... but I didn't hear him. Nasir was John the Baptist? Pete was the reason I was about to lose my Pops and the only other man I'd ever loved? I put my hand into my purse and grabbed my gun, but Nasir's arms wrapping around my waist stopped me.

"I know you're mad. I know you're surprised. I know you're hurt. Think, Meya. You're in this white ass restaurant with all these cameras. You pull your gun out and start shooting you'll be arrested before the night is over," he whispered into my ear.

"Let me go," I said as calmly as I could. He released me unwillingly. "You're John the Baptist?" I asked after I turned around to face him.

Pete sped walked out of the restaurant the minute I turned my back to him. That didn't matter. It would be nothing for me to find his ass and do away with him.

"Meya, everything that we've shared has been real. That was my job... but this that we have is personal."

I chuckled in disbelief. I was expecting him to deny the shit, but being the man that he was he owned up to it. Like it was cool. Like I would say okay that's cool and we could continue to see each other. Like he hadn't just ruined my life by putting the two men I love most against each other.

I took a step back and covered my mouth with both hands. He was right – there was no way I could get away with pulling a gun in the restaurant. I tried to walk away but his arm around my waist stopped me.

"Let me explain."

"Fuck that and fuck you. You lucky we're in this restaurant or I'd shoot your ass right now."

"Meya, you know I want you. I never wanted the business to come between us."

"Nasir, please, let me go."

"I will, but you have to hear me out."

"I don't have to hear shit!" I yelled loud enough to gain everyone in the room's attention. With a whisper I said, "You better listen to me good. You better shoot me the second we leave this restaurant because if you don't that's it for your ass. I just lost every fucking thing because of you!"

"No you haven't. Let me fix this. Let me show you that I want you. I'll give him the money back."

"Fuck the money. My pops got a price on his head because of you. Salem don't want to have shit to do with me, and if he goes through with killing my pops I have no choice but to go after him. And you think giving some fucking money back will fix that?"

"I can protect your father. Niggas might fear and respect Salem and want his money, but no one will go against John the Baptist. Let me help you."

"No, fuck that! How does Pete even know who you are? I thought no one ever saw your face? So how does he know you?"

"It's a long story. Just... let me help you. If I can protect your father will you give me a chance to show you that this was just business? I don't want to lose you, Meya. I can't lose you. You make me feel normal. Just let me fix this shit."

At this point, I knew I couldn't trust his ass, but if he had a way of protecting my pops I might have to take a chance with him.

"Give me some time to think about it."

"What is there to think about, Meya? And how much time do you think you have? How long do you think Salem is going to wait? If you want me to handle this, you need to tell me now."

"What do you mean handle it?"

He grabbed my hand and pulled me outside.

"There's a couple of ways we can do this. I can spread word in prison that if Cedrick is touched every nigga involved and his family will pay, or I can go straight to the source. Salem can't have him killed if he's no longer living himself."

"No. You leave him the hell alone. Don't touch him."

"Fine. Say the word. Tell me what you want me to do. I know you see me as your enemy right now... but you have to think logically and not emotionally. That was just business. Let me fix it. If not for us... for your father. Let me protect him. Let me fix this shit."

"Fine. Fine! Take care of this shit," I agreed.

"Thank you. I promise you won't regret this. I'm sorry, Meya. I didn't plan on approaching you or getting attached to you. It just... happened."

I nodded and tried to walk away. I didn't know how I was going to get home, but I couldn't spend another second around his ass. If he could protect my pops, I'd let him... but after that... his ass was done. Nasir grabbed my arm and kept me from walking away.

"I just need some air," I rushed out.

"Let me take you home."

"No, I'll call Kat to come get me. I just... this is too much."

"No. If you try to double cross me... I'll kill you. Simple as that. So, I think it's best that you ride with me long enough for me to convince you that my feelings for you are real."

I swallowed hard and nodded. No man's threats had ever fazed me but this man... this man was in a league of his fucking on.

"Understood," I mumbled pulling my arm away from him.

His hands covered my cheeks and he lifted my head slightly. Just the thought of him kissing me had my food rumbling in my stomach – preparing to make its way out of me. How could one of the sexiest men I'd ever known become the ugliest and most despicable being I'd ever known in a matter of seconds?

How could the presence that was just giving me such peace suddenly be robbing me of it? How could the hands and lips of the second man I'd considered sharing my life with make me want to end it and say fuck it all? His lips... his lips covered mine... and for the first time in my life I understood the pain, anger, betrayal, and shame that came from kissing and sleeping with the enemy.

To be continued...

CPSIA information can be obtained
at www.ICGtesting.com
Printed in the USA
LVOW01s0252190417
531316LV00008B/183/P